PITCHIN'
A FIT

BRANDILYN COLLINS

DEARING FAMILY SERIES
BOOK 2

ISBN: 0989240630
ISBN-13: 978-0-9892406-3-5

"Moves along briskly ... the popular novelist's talent continues to flower."

--Publishers Weekly, Gone to Ground

"A taut, heartbreaking thriller ... Collins is a fine writer who knows to both horrify readers and keep them turning pages."

--Publishers Weekly, Over the Edge

"Solidly constructed ... a strong and immediately likeable protagonist ... one of the Top 10 Inspirational Novels of 2010."

--Booklist, Deceit

"A hefty dose of action and suspense with a superb conclusion."

--RT Book Reviews, Exposure

"Intense ... engaging ... whiplash-inducing plot twists."

--Thrill Writer, Dark Pursuit

"A harrowing hostage drama."

--Library Journal, Amber Morn

"One of the Best Books of 2007 ... Top Christian suspense of the year."

--Library Journal Starred Review, Crimson Eve

"A chilling mystery ... not one to be read alone at night."

--RT BOOKclub, Coral Moon

"A sympathetic heroine ... effective flashbacks ... Collins knows how to weave faith into a rich tale."

--Library Journal, Violet Dawn

"A master storyteller ... Collins deftly finesses the accelerator on this knuckle-chomping ride."
--RT BOOKclub, Web of Lies

"Finely crafted ... vivid ... another masterpiece that keeps the reader utterly engrossed."
--RT BOOKclub, Dread Champion

"Chilling ... a confusing, twisting trail that keeps pages turning."
--Publishers Weekly, Eyes of Elisha

BOOKS BY
BRANDILYN COLLINS

Southern Contemporary

Bradleyville Series

Cast a Road Before Me
Color the Sidewalk for Me
Capture the Wind for Me

Dearing Family Series

That Dog Won't Hunt
Pitchin' a Fit

Suspense

Stand Alone Novels

Sidetracked
Dark Justice
Gone to Ground
Over the Edge
Deceit
Exposure
Dark Pursuit

**Rayne Tour YA Series
(co-written with Amberly Collins)**

Always Watching
Last Breath
Final Touch

Kanner Lake Series

Violet Dawn
Coral Moon
Crimson Eve
Amber Morn

Hidden Faces Series

Brink of Death
Stain of Guilt
Dead of Night
Web of Lies

Chelsea Adams Series

Eyes of Elisha
Dread Champion

Non-Fiction

*Getting Into Character:
Seven Secrets a Novelist Can Learn From Actors*

CHAPTER 1

Getting married wasn't supposed to be this complicated.

Twenty-three-year-old Christina Day pushed blonde hair out of her eyes and beamed a smile at the circle of women perched in the Dearings' living room. They were all older than she. And Christina didn't know anyone who'd come to her bridal shower except for her future mother-in-law, Ruth Dearing, and her three future sisters-in-law, Sarah, Maddy, and Jess, all in their thirties. Most of the other women attended New Life Church in Justus, Mississippi, where the Dearing family had worshipped for years. Christina had gone there only once. And that had been five months ago in July at the Dearing reunion, on the day the crazy family ended up posing for their annual picture on a row of old toilets — and Christina decided she could marry Ben after all.

Not that the first event directly led to the second.

Christina wanted to marry Ben more than anything. From the first day she met him at work in Dallas she'd been attracted to him. Ben was far from the stereotypical computer programmer nerd. His blue eyes could light up a room, and his friendly, boyish face and laidback attitude charmed everyone. Their wedding would be wonderful and simple, just the way Christina wanted it. The next two days would produce memories for a lifetime.

She just had to get through them first.

"You okay?" Ruth Dearing mouthed to Christina from across the room.

Oh, no. Christina gave her a big nod and smiled. Had some expression given her away? Mama Ruth was so compassionate. She'd gone to a lot of trouble to throw this bridal shower in her own home. Today was December fifth, yet she'd held off putting up a Christmas tree to make room for all the women. Still, she seemed so aware it may not be the easiest thing for Christina. Ruth Dearing deserved to see only happiness on the face of her almost daughter-in-law. Both Mama Ruth and her husband, Syton, had been nothing but kind to Christina. And she hadn't always deserved it.

"Oh, look at that beautiful wrapping." A large woman seated on the sofa pointed to the purple and gold covered gift Christina held. The woman had introduced herself rather importantly as the police chief's wife. Dana ... Something. "Did you do that yourself, Patricia?"

"Sure did." Miss Patricia smiled at Christina, showing dentured teeth. She had to be at least in her 70s. Her face was heavily powdered, which only accentuated her wrinkles. But a light of love and acceptance shone in her eyes. Patricia Bigslow had proudly told Christina she served as the church pianist. "I think a pretty wrapping's half the fun, don't you?"

"Yes," Christina said. "It is really pretty."

She repressed a wince. Why did her responses have to sound so formal and *lame*? These women were going out of their way to welcome her into the Dearing family. They could have just brought their gifts to the wedding on Saturday, but they'd given up a Thursday night to honor her.

Christina slipped scissors beneath the gold ribbon and cut it. She handed the large bow to Maddy, on her left, who pulled the ribbon ends through a hole cut in the middle of a white paper plate, leaving the bow to crowd with all the others on top. Maddy had informed Christina this would serve as her "bouquet" at tomorrow night's rehearsal. A tradition Christina had never heard of.

"Careful." Miss Patricia leaned forward. "It's breakable."

"Okay." Christina removed the box's lid. Inside sat a blue and white serving bowl, one she and Ben had chosen for their gift registry. "Oh." Gratitude welled within her. "Thank you so much. It's a piece we really wanted."

"You're welcome." Miss Patricia laid a hand against her cheek. "My own daughter chose a pattern a lot like that. Brings back memories of her wedding."

The words pierced Christina. Mother and daughter— together at a wedding.

On cue, the well-worn memories rushed her. The beatings ... the dark locked closet. Christina's eyes burned. She dropped her gaze and steeled herself. Shoved the memories down.

Help me, Jesus.

Raising her head, Christina smiled as she waited for Sarah to note the gift and giver, then handed her the box. Soon all the ladies were admiring the bowl as they passed it around the circle.

3

Jess got up from her seat next to Maddy and chose another gift from the table to bring to Christina. She still had over a dozen to open.

"You worn out yet?" Jess grinned down at her. Typical blunt Jessica. She'd been the hardest person in the Dearing family to get along with during the summer reunion. But she and Christina had worked on their relationship since then. Jess had forgiven Christina for the soapy-lobsters-in-the-sink fiasco. But whenever Sarah and Maddy teased her about it she still got all red in the face.

"How could I be worn out, opening all these wonderful presents?" Christina smiled up at Jess. Her lips were feeling more brittle by the minute.

Jess gave her a look that said *I can see right through you, girl, and I know you're miserable.*

Christina glanced away. She wasn't miserable. It was just ... all these new people. And the constant chatter. So hard for someone who'd learned to draw inward out of self defense.

But she didn't have to do that anymore.

Another present, and another. More bows through the plate and ripped paper on the floor. More smiles and laughter, and comments from the sweet Mississippi women about their own weddings, and their sons' and daughters'.

So far not one person had asked about Christina's own family—normally the polite Southern thing to do. No doubt they'd been warned by Ruth to stay away from the subject. Her father had died from a heart attack eighteen months ago—after years of heavy drinking. And how to explain why her own mother wasn't invited to the wedding? Hadn't even been *told* about it. Just the thought of her in-your-face alcoholic mother here with all these proper ladies made Christina shudder.

4

She opened the rest of her gifts, all from her registry list. Christina pictured herself moved into Ben's apartment with all their new stuff. It would be so perfect.

"Phew." Maddy stuck a hand in her long chestnut hair. "Looks like that's it. The train has left the building."

Jess and Sarah chortled.

Oh, boy. Another one of Maddy's mixed metaphors. Her sisters wouldn't let her get away with it.

Maddy frowned at Jess. "What are you cacklin' at?"

"The train's left the building, Maddy?" Jess stuck out her chin. "Is that sorta like—Elvis has left the station?"

Titters went around the circle. Even Mama Ruth laughed. Maddy just huffed. "Oh, for heaven's sake, you know what I mean."

The three sisters exchanged looks. Christina's heart twinged. To have sisters like that. So much history together. They could tease and argue and love all at the same time. Something Christina hadn't understood at first.

"All right, everyone." Ruth stood. "Thank you so much for your wonderful gifts. Now we have refreshments in the dinin' room."

Christina's thoughts flashed to Penny, the Dearings' Yorkie. The tiny dog had been closed off in the family room for some time now. Lady Penelope—her full name—was probably curled up in her fluffy yellow bed. By now she'd be totally ticked off, as only a Yorkie who considered herself royalty could be. In Penny's mind, *she* owned the house, not the humans, and all too often they required her to put up with things completely beneath her.

If Christina got the chance, she'd slip into the family room and check on her.

Christina looked around the circle at all the women. "Thank you very much. You've been so kind to me, and I'm grateful."

The woman next to Sarah beamed. "And we're so glad to see you join the Dearing family."

Everyone murmured agreement.

"Okay!" Jess tossed back her shoulder-length blonde hair. "Let's eat, I'm starved."

They gathered around Ruth's dining room table for little sandwiches and cakes and punch, all made by Ruth with the help of Jess, Sarah, and Maddy. More love in action to welcome Christina into the family. The mere thought made her want to cry.

The women's voices and punch cups swirled and tinkled. Again and again Christina smiled and repeated her thank-yous. How long before she could just be alone with Ben? He had a way of helping her chill out. But for now the Dearing men and sons-in-law had taken off to have supper in Jackson, Maddy's daughter and Sarah's two kids in tow.

"Christina's a real beauty, isn't she," a woman with pink cheeks remarked to another. They stood by the front dining room window, dainty plates in their hands. What were their names again?

"She certainly is." The second woman raised a bite of cake to her red lips. "Ben's a lucky young man."

"Who do you think you are, Ugly Bug?" The sneering face of Christina's father rose in her mind. *"You'll never amount to nothin'."*

Across the room Miss Patricia chattered a mile a minute with the pastor's wife, Judy Crenshaw. Miss Judy would be leading the dress rehearsal on Friday. She was pretty—in her mid-forties maybe. Her hair was cut short and stylish, and tinged with reddish streaks.

Christina made out Patricia's words "hollered like a stuck pig." The pastor's wife laughed.

Mama Ruth, ever the hostess, was refilling the punch bowl. Sarah, Maddy, and Jess were scattered around the living room, talking with guests. For a moment Christina found herself standing alone.

She exhaled.

The police chief's wife pattered over, carrying her plate. Oh, boy. Christina had heard from Mama Ruth that Miss Dana was a "feisty woman with the gift of gab." She was almost as wide as she was tall. Her brown hair was Southern big, teased and in layered flips. Her long red nails were perfectly done, and her glitzy earrings, necklace, and bracelet all matched. "Poor thing, you feelin' a little overwhelmed, bein' out of your own stompin' grounds?" Miss Dana's voice was loud enough to carry across the room.

Christina's lips curved. "Oh, no. Everyone has made me feel so at home."

"Well, the Dearings are a wonderful family. Everyone in Justus loves 'em."

"Me too."

Awkward silence. Miss Dana studied Christina's face. "Where are you and Ben goin' on your honeymoon?"

"To Cabo San Lucas. It's a real pretty resort."

"Oh, my, sounds lovely. I suppose it's warm in December."

"Yes. In the seventies."

Miss Dana nodded. "Well, my husband, Ronald Altweather—everyone calls him Buddy, he's the police chief, you know—his brother went to Cabo once. Said it was so pretty he hardly wanted to come back home."

Christina nodded.

Miss Dana took a sip of punch and set the cup back on her plate. "Mm. That's good."

"Yes. It's wonderful."

Miss Dana tilted her head up at Christina. "Sorry your mama couldn't be with you tonight. I take it she's comin' to the weddin'?"

Christina's head buzzed. In the dining room—sudden silence. Heads turned toward them, shaking in *oh-no*, bodies stilling. Patricia's mouth stopped mid-chew. The women's reactions were almost worse than Christina's frozen throat. They *had* been warned, which meant they knew about her mother. Except for Dana Altweather, who apparently didn't get the memo. Shame rattled up Christina's spine. "Well, I—"

"Dana, how 'bout you helpin' me in the kitchen for a minute." Mama Ruth appeared out of nowhere and placed a gentle hand on the woman's back.

Miss Dana frowned, clearly confused at the stir her question had caused. "All right." She nodded to Christina and allowed herself to be ushered away.

Christina's heart fluttered. So many eyes on her. See? She *wasn't* good enough to be here with these people. Surely none of them came from the kind of background she did.

She wanted to melt through the floor.

Miss Judy stepped forward. "Say, Christina, I've got an idea. Why don't you show us your weddin' dress?"

Relieved nods and fervent yesses all around. The women were in dire need for a change of subject.

Christina swallowed. "Now? Before the wedding?"

"Sure enough, honey chil'." Miss Judy grinned. "I don't see any men-folk around. So bring it on out, let us ooh and ahh. A little birdie told me it's beautiful." She winked at Jess.

Jess said that?

"That's a great idea." Sarah took Christina's arm. "Let's go get it."

8

Christina wouldn't say no to Sarah. Ben's oldest sister had been a calming help to her at the July reunion.

The next thing she knew, she was being led down the east wing hallway toward the lovely red and gold guest room, where the wedding dress hung in the closet. Encased in a white plastic covering, it had filled an entire suitcase on their flight from Dallas.

As they passed the closed pocket door to the family room, Christina stopped. "I should check on Penny."

Sarah twisted her mouth. "You know she's gonna be mad."

"I know. I thought I'd —"

"She takes one look at you, and she'll give you the Lady Penelope treatment."

Christina pictured the Yorkie stalking to the corner and sticking her little nose in it, her back to the room. Penny's way of saying, *I certainly will not interact with you after the despicable way I've been treated.*

"And then," — Sarah tilted her head — "when you leave her *again* she'll be doubly mad."

Christina sighed. Why couldn't people — and dogs — just be easy? "Okay." She tried to smile, but it came out crooked.

Sarah peered at her. "You all right?"

Of course she was all right. This was her wedding shower. So what if someone had mentioned her mother — and the entire room stood still. "Yeah."

Sarah patted her arm. "Don't worry about it. Dana will feel terrible when she hears."

That was just it. The mere mention of her mother made people feel terrible. Tears brimmed in Christina's eyes.

"Oh no, don't cry. I'm so sorry." Sarah pulled her into a hug. "I can't imagine how hard it is for you. Now, of all times." She stepped back and laid her hands on

9

Christina's cheeks. "Just know you've got a mother now in my mama. She already loves you like a daughter."

"I know."

Still, Mama Ruth wasn't her *real* mother. Her real mother had stood by and watched while Christina's father beat her. Had done nothing when he threw her into a closet or treated her like a slave. Now in her early fifties and a widow, Edna Day dressed in revealing clothes and chased any man with two legs. The woman still cared for absolutely no one but herself.

Christina took a deep breath and blinked away the tears. "I'm sorry."

Sarah shook her head. "Nothin' to be sorry for." She shot Christina an impish grin. "Come on now. Let's show those women what a stunnin' dress you've got."

"Okay."

It *was* stunning, even though Christina had bought it at a bargain price. A few minutes later in the living room, surrounded by all the women, Christina unzipped the plastic bag with Sarah's help and pulled out the dress.

"Ohhh!" The women's mouths rounded. "It's wonderful!"

"So different!"

"Look at those curlicue decorations."

"My goodness, I've never seen such an elegant gown."

"Honey, Ben's just gonna *die*." Miss Judy held up both palms.

The dress was strapless and fitted at the waist, with a full skirt made of white panels that parted to show white and black swirling designs underneath. Matching designs adorned the bodice. It was princessy and Southern and modern all at once. Christina had never seen a dress like it. She would carry a bouquet of red roses to add vivid color—and in honor of the Christmas season.

"I can't wait to see her in it." Mama Ruth's face beamed. "Just seein' it on the hanger is breathtakin'."

Sudden headlights appeared on the street. Christina peered through the front windows and saw a car pulling half into the already full driveway.

"Oh!" She grabbed for the dress's hanging bag. "Ben and the men are back. They'll have to come through the front door."

Mama Ruth frowned. "What're they doin' here so soon?" She and Sarah started to put the dress back into its container.

"Wait." Sarah bent down. "One of the panels is gettin' crushed."

Christina knew the skirt was too big to fit in the bag easily. "Take it out and start again." She glanced through the window. A figure was heading toward the porch. "Hurry!"

"I'll head them off at the pass." Mama Ruth turned toward the entryway. "They'll just have to wait on the cold porch till we're done—that's what they get for comin' back so soon."

The women gathered in front of Christina and the dress. "Don't worry," someone said. "Those men aren't gonna see through us, even if they do get in."

Miss Dana laughed. "They won't see through *me*, that's for sure."

The dress lay in the bag for the second time. Christina carefully pushed in the skirt, then reached to bring the sides of the bag over it. She heard Mama Ruth throw open the front door and declare, "Hold it right—"

"Well, looky there!" The raucous voice of a years-long female smoker called from the porch.

Christina froze.

"I didn't even have to ring the doorbell!" The woman emitted a hard laugh—one Christina knew all too well.

The tingling started in her hands. Scurried up her arms and down her body. Christina turned toward the door. Over two dozen pairs of eyes caught her horrified expression and followed her gaze.

"Oh." Mama Ruth sounded flustered. "I'm sorry. I didn't—"

"I *know* you weren't expectin' me. None of y'all was." Accusation coated the words.

Christina couldn't breathe.

"I think you got a girl here named Christina Day. Gettin' married on Saturday? Well, I'm her mama. The one she 'forgot' to invite."

CHAPTER 2

Oh, dear Lord, help us all.

Ruth Dearing shot a look at Christina. She looked sickly pale. The horror stories Ruth had heard about the woman now standing on her porch flashed in her mind.

She turned back to Edna Day. The woman stood about Ruth's height—five-two—with hands on her hips. Her faded jeans looked skin-tight on her slender frame and were tucked into glittery boots. Her black jacket was unzipped, revealing a beige sweater cut embarrassingly low. Edna's short flame-red hair stuck straight up. She wore heavy make-up and an attitude that could pulse through walls.

"Well. How nice." Ruth tried to keep her voice from wavering. "Can I—"

Edna pushed past her into the entryway. She reeked of cigarette smoke.

Dread silence wafted from the living room. Every woman took in Edna—and widened her eyes. Jess looked the woman up and down and curled her lip.

Edna stopped at the threshold of the living room and regarded the scene. The front of the wedding dress still showed from inside the hanging bag. She eyed it. *"Black?* On a *weddin'* dress?" She laughed, a grating, caustic sound. "What kinda life you been livin', Chris?"

From the closed off family room, Lady Penelope barked. Ruth blinked. Penny *never* barked.

Ruth could see Christina's chest rise and fall with fitful breathing. Ruth moved beside Edna. She had to *do* something.

Edna rested her weight on one leg, pushing out her hip. She gestured with her chin toward her daughter. "Ain't you even gonna say hello?"

Christina didn't move.

Ruth stepped into the living room. "Actually, we were—"

"Havin' a party, obviously." Edna tilted her head, swinging long purple earrings. "A shower. Somethin' a mother should be part of." She turned a hard gaze on Ruth. "Don't you agree?"

"Mom, stop it." Christina's words cut through the living room.

Edna swung to face her. "Stop it? *Stop* it? *You're* the one who didn't even tell me you were gettin' married. You know how I heard it? From my stinkin' sister, who threw the words in my face." Edna wagged her head. "'Guess what, little sister, your daughter's gettin' married and didn't even *tell* you. Guess she loves you a *whole* lot, huh.'"

Christina's eyes filled with tears. Sarah let go of the dress bag and slipped an arm around her.

Ruth laid a hand on Edna's arm. "Let's not—"

"Let's not *what?*" Edna jerked her arm away. "What should I do, wait till after the weddin'?" She pointed at

14

Ruth. Her nails were long and sparkly purple. *"You* did this to me. You're *stealin'* my daughter."

"Oh, no, I—"

"Hey." Jess pushed through gaping women and stomped across the room to tower over Edna. Her cheeks were pink. "You *cannot* come into my mother's house and talk to her like that."

Edna smirked. "And just who are you, Miss Annie-Get-Your-Gun?"

Jess narrowed her green eyes. "Jessica Dearing, for your information. Your daughter's new sister. Part of the new family she never had."

Pain cinched Edna's face, then disappeared. Had Ruth even seen it at all?

"Edna, please." Ruth reached for her again. "Let's go in the other room and talk."

Edna's jaw hardened. "I got nothin' to say to you." She swept her hand toward the living room. *"Any* of you. Only to my daughter." She moved forward to Christina. The steel fell out of her voice. "I'm stayin' here for the weekend, Chris. I wanna see you walk down that aisle." She pointed to the dress. "Whatever crazy color you're in." Edna drew back her head. "As for the rest of y'all starin' at me, get over it. I ain't got cooties." She yanked off her jacket and threw it on the floor. Her sweater was tight and see-through, showing a black lace bra that failed to cover half of her bulging chest.

Patricia Bigslow's eyes rounded.

"You think you're stayin' in *this house?"* Jess tossed the words at Edna's back.

Edna whirled around. "Who said I'd wanna stay here with the likes of you? I got a room at the motel across town."

"Please, Edna." Ruth tried to smile at her. "Let's go in the kitchen and talk."

"What would you and me possibly have to talk about?"

Dear God, what do I do? Somehow Ruth had to calm this woman and protect Christina at the same time. "I can tell you about our family. You can tell me … about yours."

Edna snickered. "Oh, I'm sure y'all have heard all about mine. I'll bet Chris has given you an earful."

"Mom." Christina looked like she could barely breathe. "Let's go … somewhere. You and I can talk —"

Her words pinched off. Ruth knew the last thing Christina wanted was to be alone with Edna Day. But the shame of her mother's making a scene in front of all these women was even worse. Ruth caught Christina's eye — *It's all right.*

Patricia moved to Christina and patted her shoulder. "I think that's a wonderful idea, honey." She turned a smile on Edna.

"Y'all shouldn't have to go anywhere." Judy Crenshaw spoke up. "We can leave. Right, girls? Then you can sit in here and talk. Ruthie, I'll help you get everyone's coat."

"Yes, yes." Dana Altweather flapped a beefy hand. "That's what we should do." All business, she bustled after Judy toward the hall. As she passed Edna, she mustered what Ruth knew to be the epitome of her Southern politeness. "Nice to meet you."

"*Thank* you." Edna snapped the words and gave her daughter a look. "See? At least somebody around here has some manners."

Dana slowed, as if deciding upon a retort. Clearly she hadn't meant her words to be used against Christina.

Ruth shook her head.

Dana moved on.

16

Ruth, Judy, and Dana hurried to Sarah's and Jake's bedroom, where coats were piled on the bed. Patricia joined them.

Judy laid a hand against her cheek. "Oh, Ruthie, she's *horrible*. What are we gonna *do*?"

Ruth was sick to the pit of her stomach. "I don't know. This is Christina's worst nightmare. She and Ben chose to get married here instead of Dallas just so her mother wouldn't have a chance of showin' up—even though it meant a lot of their friends wouldn't be here. This just isn't *fair*."

Patricia scooped up four coats. "Maybe you can convince her to leave."

"How? I can't tell a mother to leave her own daughter's weddin'."

"But if she's not wanted ..."

"That's just it." Ruth held out both arms while Dana loaded them up with jackets. "Can't you see the hurt on her face? I mean, if you look past all the anger. She *wants* to be wanted."

Dana tsked. "Nice way of showin' it. Some people don't deserve to be wanted." She wagged her head. "And I'm sorry again that I mentioned her to Christina. Poor girl."

Judy wagged her head in her teasing way. "Yeah, look what you did, Dana, you went and conjured the woman up."

Dana made a sound in her throat. "Do go on."

Patricia headed for the hallway. "You're right, Ruthie. It's just ... we're all gonna have to help Christina. It could be a long weekend."

No kidding. Especially with Jess and Edna anywhere near each other. Ruth knew her youngest daughter. She'd gotten her back up at the woman—and it would stay there.

17

They filed down the hall, laden with coats. In the living room Sarah and Christina were zipping up the wedding dress's hanging bag. Christina still looked pale. Edna sat on a love seat, legs crossed, watching. Maddy sat beside her, lacing and unlacing her hands, clearly searching for something to say. Women were offering their goodbyes and best wishes to Christina—and nodding to her mother. At sight of the coats there was a mad rush to unite with the right one and get out the door. Ruth emptied her arms and went back for more.

Christina followed, carrying the wedding dress. They stopped in the hall outside Sarah's door.

Ruth touched Christina's arm. "How are you?"

Christina hesitated, then shook her head.

Ruth's heart ached. "I'm so sorry."

"*I'm* sorry." Christina's voice was tight. "I can't believe this is happening. I never wanted her here."

"I know."

"But you *don't*! You don't know how bad she can be. This, tonight? She's *sober*."

Ruth swallowed. "She won't hurt you, will she? I mean physically."

Christina pressed her lips together. "No."

She started to say more, then closed her mouth. After a moment she turned toward the guest room to hang up the dress.

"I'll be with you through whatever happens," Ruth whispered after her. "So will Ben. All of us."

"Thanks."

Ben would hit the roof. He was the one who'd told Ruth about Edna. Usually easygoing, every ounce of his protectiveness had surfaced just in relating the stories of abuse.

Ruth fetched the last of the coats while Christina hung up her dress. They walked back toward the living

18

room together. The front door hung open, many of the shower guests already heading to their cars. "Thank you, all of you," Ruth said to those who remained. With hands full she couldn't hug any of them.

Patricia slid an arm around her shoulder. "We'll be prayin' for y'all." She kept her voice low.

Ruth nodded.

Christina stayed near the door, thanking the women as they left. Ruth knew she was delaying having to face her mother. Edna was now on her feet, pacing. She and Jess eyed one another across the living room like prowling tigers.

"Did you drive all the way here from ... where is it you live?" Ruth heard Sarah ask Edna. That was Sarah's nature—trying to reach out. Find common ground, hard as that would be in this case.

"Austin. And yes, I drove. Took me *all day*. Hard to find this tiny little town. And I had to ask someone where this house was. But anything for my daughter."

Sarah couldn't seem to find a reply.

The last guest gone, Ruth and Christina reluctantly returned to the living room. Jess had disappeared. Maddy and Sarah were picking up wrapping paper and stuffing it into a large plastic trash bag. Edna was admiring the display of gifts, running the tip of her finger around a pretty plate.

Dense silence hung in the air.

Edna let out a sigh and turned. "Well, here, let me help." She started gathering paper. When her hands were full she straightened and gazed at the colorful pieces she held. Her face pinched.

Ruth looked to Christina. Her back seemed wooden, her fingers curled. But something flicked across her expression as she watched her mother react to the

19

tattered remains of a wedding shower she had not attended. Sadness? Remorse? Longing?

Edna caught her daughter's gaze. Her face shuttered. "I should have been here. You had no right to cut me out."

Maddy's eyelids flickered. She shoved a strand of hair off her cheek and continued her work with vehemence.

Ruth squeezed Christina's arm. "Edna, maybe the three of us can talk? Would you like somethin' to drink or eat first?"

Edna sneered. "Like I said, I got nothin' to talk about with *you*. You're the one tryin' to steal my daughter from me." She stuffed the paper into the plastic sack.

"She's not stealing me!" Christina sat down hard on the couch, as if her legs would no longer hold her.

"Then what do you call this?" Edna swept out her hand.

Christina's eyes glistened. "I just wanted to get married in peace."

"And you can't do that with me here?"

Christina's mouth opened, then closed.

"Well, you can't throw me outta town. I'm here till I see you hitched. So don't be figurin' how to get rid of me, 'cause it ain't gonna work." Edna shook her head. "You're stuck with me, Ugly Bug."

CHAPTER 3

Ben leaned against the bench in the noisy pizza parlor in Jackson, arms stretched out on either side. His right hand curled around his dad's shoulder. With his left he playfully tugged at his niece Lacey's brown ringlets. Lacey, age six, grinned up at him. She and her five-year-old cousin, Alex, who sat across the table, could hardly keep still. Too much excitement this weekend. Both of them were flower girls in the wedding. And Pogey, Lacey's ten-year-old brother who was now chowing down on his fourth piece of pizza at the end of the table, would be ring bearer. Pogey was thrilled.

Not.

No worries, the kid would come around. He absolutely loved Christina, and she'd asked him to be in the wedding, thinking he wouldn't want to be left out. So she was wrong. Her heart was in the right place.

Ben looked around at his wonderful family and grinned. His belly was full and his heart fuller. He could hardly believe his wedding weekend was finally here.

21

"Anyone want dessert?" Their waitress started to clear plates. "We got a chocolate cake to die for."

"Absolutely." Ben flashed her a smile. "Bring it on."

His dad gave him a look. "Aren't you the big spender."

"Me? I thought *you* were payin'."

Syton Dearing feigned surprise, but his blue eyes sparkled. "Hey, I'm just a retired old man." He gestured with his chin across the table to Don Dexter, Maddy's husband. "No, wait. Weren't *you* payin'?"

Don ran a hand over his buzz cut blond hair, as if trying to remember. "Wasn't me said that. It was Jake."

Sarah's husband. An insurance salesman who looked the part, with his black hair, wire rim glasses and tall nerdiness.

Jake reached for his wallet. "You're right, I did."

"You did not." Ben's dad shook his head. "Put that thing away. "

Ben poked his shoulder. "I thought we were goin' Dutch."

"No, Daddy," Lacey announced to Jake. "Alex and me are payin'."

"But I don't have any money!" Alex raised one of her famous pouts.

Don leaned his elbows on the table. "Well, I guess you two will have to dance for quarters."

Alex gave him an imperial look. "*I* don't dance, Daddy."

"I do!" Lacey raised her eyebrows. "I can show 'em my ballet steps!"

"Like anybody'd pay for that." Alex rolled her eyes.

Lacey's lips turned down. "Well, maybe somebody would."

"'Course they would." Don frowned at his daughter. "That wasn't very nice."

Alex was suddenly very interested in her glass of Coke.

The chocolate cake arrived. It looked almost as good as Mom's. Ben picked up his fork and dug in.

His cell phone rang.

He fished it out of his pocket. Jess's name appeared on the screen.

Ben's dad peered at the name. "Home callin'. Probably sayin' the menfolk can come back now. Little ones too." He reached across the table and tweaked Alex's nose.

Ben put the phone to his ear. "Hi, Jess."

She started talking a mile a minute, but the restaurant was too loud. All the same, he caught the tone of her voice. His sister was royally ticked about something.

"Wait, I can't hear you. Let me go outside."

"Hurry up!" Jess shouted.

Ben motioned for his dad to slide off the bench so he could get up. He hurried across the old wooden floor of the pizza parlor and out the front door. It was cold outside for December, in the low forties. He drew in his shoulders. "What's goin' on?"

"Not what, *who*. As in your future mother-in-law." Jess's voice could have cut metal.

Ben stilled. "What about her?"

"She's *here*. Arrived on the porch and broke up the shower in a hurry. Says she's not gonna miss the weddin'."

Ben's veins froze. No. No way. The very thing Christina dreaded most.

"You gotta get home, Ben. Right now."

Of course he did. "How's Christina?"

"Stunned. Ashamed. Her mom looks like a total slut. Acts like one too. Christina told you she was bad? She's *worse*."

23

Oh, man. No, no, no.

"You shoulda heard the things she said in front of all those guests! And to Mom! I about slapped her upside the head."

Ben could imagine. He'd never wanted to meet Christina's mother. After all the stories he'd heard, he despised the woman.

How in the world would his fiancée handle this? She'd been through a lot of counseling in the past five months, but *this*. No way was she ready for it. "Where's Christina?"

"In the livin' room with Punk Medusa. Mom and Sarah and Maddy are in there too. I snuck into the kitchen to call you. Even Penny's all upset. Hear her barkin'? When have you *ever* heard Lady Penelope bark? Only canines do that."

Ben did hear Penny. Her yips sounded high and squeaky—and quite offended.

He put a hand to his forehead. "Okay. I'll fix this. She's not stayin' here, no way. I'll *make* her leave."

"Yeah, well, lotsa luck tryin'. That woman clearly doesn't think about anybody but herself. She's got Christina in tears, and does she care?"

Christina in tears, two days before her wedding. This was a nightmare.

"And, Ben, *I'm* tellin' *you* she's not settin' foot at your weddin', 'cause I'll *kill* her before it ever gets here!"

His sister would, too. Edna Day by herself was enough to cause fireworks. Pair her with Jess ...

"Okay, okay, calm down." Ben turned with purpose toward the restaurant. "Be there soon as I can." The trip home would be the longest thirty-five minutes he ever spent. "Tell Christina I'm comin'."

Ben clicked off the call and yanked open the pizza parlor door.

24

CHAPTER 4

Ugly Bug. Christina flinched at the old name. Memories of her father's sneering face rushed her.

"Edna." Mama Ruth's voice was firm. "Please don't call her that."

"Why not?" Edna spread her red lips wide. "It was her dad's favorite name for her."

Seated on the couch, Christina blinked up at her mother. "Yeah, I know. And it *hurt.*"

Christina's own voice shocked her. She'd never talked back to her mother like that.

But how could the woman not understand? She couldn't possibly believe a nickname like Ugly Bug would make her daughter feel good. Feel loved. How could a mother let her daughter be called that? Over the years those two words had drilled every bit of self esteem Christina could have possessed right out of her. Until she'd thought—no, knew: *I'm ugly. Unlovable. As low as a roach.*

Her mother stared back as if surprised, then raised a shoulder. "You always were so sensitive."

Christina could feel anger spilling off Mama Ruth. Sarah and Maddy exchanged disgusted looks. Sarah pushed the last bit of wrapping paper into the trash bag—hard. Stiff-fingered, Maddy tied the top of the bag. They both stood tight-mouthed, looking from Christina to her mother.

Good thing Jess wasn't in the room. She was the lawyer of the family and had no problem saying whatever she thought.

As if Christina's thoughts had summoned her, Jessica appeared in the living room doorway. She drew to a halt, taking in the frozen faces. Then focused on Christina. "Ben's on his way."

Thank goodness. Although what he'd do Christina had no clue. Ben was a take-it-easy guy and got along with everybody. Tended to see the world through rose-colored glasses, as his mother put it. Only one thing had raised his temper in Christina's presence—stories of her childhood. Ben couldn't understand how her parents had treated her so horribly.

Christina's mother raised a mock-victorious arm. "Prince to the rescue! Bet he's thrilled I'm here."

"Nobody's thrilled you're here, okay?" Jess chewed the words. "Least of all Christina. If you had any decency at all, you'd turn around and head back to the rock you slithered out from."

Edna glared at her.

Mama Ruth reached for her daughter's arm. "Jess, don't."

"Don't *what*, Mom? Like she can't see she's not wanted here?"

"I don't know why y'all hate me so much." Edna jabbed a finger toward Jess. "But I do know you can't scare me. I've been through far worse things in my life than the likes of you."

Jess's face reddened. "Maybe that's 'cause you haven't seen me in action yet."

"Don't you say another word to me, you—"

"*Stop!*" Mama Ruth held up her palms. She took a deep breath. "Jess, be quiet. Edna. You ... surprised us, that's all."

Christina's mom cursed. "Yeah, no kiddin'."

Mama Ruth's jaw firmed. "Look. I don't want to get between a mother and daughter. If you two can talk through this—fine. But no matter *who* you are, right now I don't like your attitude or the way you're talkin'. This is *my* house. You are here because I'm allowing you to be here. And that could change real fast."

Christina glanced at Jess, whose wide eyes had a shocked *you-go-Mom!* expression.

"Is that understood?" Mama Ruth raised her eyebrows.

Christina's throat swelled. She'd never heard the sweet woman talk like that to anyone. Didn't even know she could. Did she have any idea what this could unleash in Edna Day?

Her mother stared back at Mama Ruth. A long moment ticked by. Amazingly then, her face softened a little.

"Yeah. I get it."

Relief flattened Mama Ruth's expression. She nodded. "Good."

"Well, that was easy as cake." Maddy's comment was half under her breath.

"A *piece* of cake, Maddy." Sarah kept her eyes on Edna.

"Maybe she meant easy as pie," said Jess.

27

Christina's mother looked at the three sisters like they were crazy.

The room fell quiet.

"Fine then." She spread her hands. "Now that we're all nicey-nice and you three are talkin' nonsense, I want some time alone with my daughter."

"I don't think so." Jess shook her head.

Mama Ruth looked to Christina. "I'm not sure she's ready for that."

No. I'm not.

"Well, why don't we ask *her*? Seein' as how she's sittin' right here." Edna turned to Christina. "How about it? Think you could give your own mother a little of your time?"

The words were meant to be sarcastic, Christina knew. But halfway through, her mother's tone fuzzed. Almost as if she ... *cared.*

When had she ever shown that before?

Edna tilted her head. "Come on, Chris. You can't even *talk* to me?"

In an instant the old resentment surged. If it wasn't Ugly Bug it was Chris—the boy her father had wanted instead of her. "My name is *not* Chris."

Her mother raised a hand in exasperation. "Really. So just what *am* I supposed to call you?"

"Christina. My name. I'm not a boy. I'm not a bug. I'm *me.* Christina."

"Okay. *Christina.* Can we talk now?"

Jess bugged her eyes at Mama Ruth. "*Why* are we lettin' her stay here?"

"Nobody asked *you*." Christina's mother shot her a look.

Jess started to retort, but Mama Ruth cut her off. "Wait now." She took a quick breath. "Both of you just ... be quiet."

She looked to Christina. "Do you want to do this?"

Christina focused on her lap. *No, no, no, no, no!*

But if they threw her mother out, Edna Day wouldn't give up easily. She might leave this house but not the town, just like she'd threatened. Sure as you're living she'd show up at the ceremony—madder than ever. Who knew what she might pull there, in front of a church full of guests. Her shower entrance would pale by comparison. And Christina's wedding—the day she had longed for since she was a small, desperate child—would be ruined.

One hard lesson Christina had learned from her abusive childhood—do anything to keep the peace. Stuff down your emotions. Shove 'em in a box and nail down the lid. Do what's expected—because the tiniest infraction could mean disaster.

She had to say *yes*.

But Christina was no longer a child trapped in her parents' house. She'd been in counseling for the past five months. She was trying to break free of the past, be a new person.

She should say *no*.

But her mother was still the same person. And that's what mattered.

Christina's lungs burned. She was about to be married, looking forward to a new life. But here again—the same old trap.

Will I ever be free of this, God?

She took a deep breath and raised her chin. "Yes. We can talk."

Jess flicked a look at the ceiling.

Mama Ruth regarded Christina, as if asking, *You sure?*

She nodded.

The silence pulsed.

"Okay." Mama Ruth sounded reticent. "We'll go in the kitchen and let you two … work things out." Her final words mixed doubt and hope. "Christina, we're here if you need us."

Edna spread her hands. "What, like I'm some criminal or somethin'?"

Jess's mouth opened. Mama Ruth shook her head sternly. "Let's go." She motioned to her daughters.

Maddy turned to follow, looking grim. Sarah moved to the couch and leaned down to place her palms on Christina's cheeks. She gave Christina a smile and a nod—*you can do this.*

Christina hoped Sarah could see the gratitude in her eyes.

Jess was the last one out of the living room. Before disappearing around the corner she shot Christina's mom a hard look.

Edna scowled at her.

In the next moment the Dearing women were gone. Leaving Christina to face her mother.

Alone.

CHAPTER 5

"Why'd you *do* that?" Jess faced her mother in the kitchen. "Christina looks like a deer in headlights out there!"

"Shh, they'll hear you." Ruth held Penny, who'd run over the minute they entered the room, her little pink-banded topknot bouncing. At least the Yorkie had stopped barking. The silk of her blonde-beige coat felt comforting in Ruth's fingers.

"Who cares if she hears me? We *have* to get that woman out of here!"

"She's wretched, Mama." Maddy tossed back her hair. "Truly wretched."

Jess wagged her head. "I got worse words for her."

Sarah put an arm around their mother's shoulder. "Y'all calm down now, really. This isn't easy for Mama either."

No kidding. But Ruth's main worry lay with Christina. Had she done the right thing, allowing Edna to stay? *Please, God, yes. Help us all.*

Ruth glanced at the oven clock. Not long now before Syton and the other men got home. Thank goodness. But when Ben stepped foot in the house, would that make things better or worse?

Jess returned to the closed pocket door leading to the dining room and leaned her ear against the wood.

"Hear anything?" Maddy whispered.

Jess shook her head. "A word now and then." She straightened. "So what are we gonna do?"

Penny wiggled in Ruth's arms. Ruth ran her hand over the dog's back. "Calm down, girl."

"Mama?" Jess folded her arms.

The phone rang.

Ruth's shoulders slumped. "Let it be. We got enough goin' on."

"Maybe it's Ben." Jess headed for the phone and peered at the ID. "No, it's Tamel." She snatched up the receiver.

Tamel Curd, Jess's boyfriend. The man who'd given up his law practice to return to Justus and nurse his ailing father. Jess and Tamel had grown up together. She'd claimed she couldn't stand him—until soapy lobster day last summer, when Jess and Christina had their fight and the whole house was in an uproar.

"Tamel, you're not gonna believe what happened." Jess didn't bother to say *hello*. "The Wicked Witch of the West just showed up." Jess headed into the family room and plopped into a chair, spilling words of venom about Edna Day.

Sarah patted Ruth's shoulder. "You okay?"

"I'm fine. It's Christina I'm worried about."

"Yeah. Well. Maybe this talk will do them good."

Ruth shook her head. "I don't know. It could be a disaster. I wanted to throw her out. But it's not that simple. Awful as she was—*is*—there's somethin' about

32

her, did you see it? A flicker now and then. I think she's very hurt that she wasn't invited to the weddin'. I think she desperately wants her daughter to *want* her."

Maddy lifted a hand, palm up. "How could Christina want her around, after the terrible way she treated her?"

"I know, I know."

"It's like the woman doesn't have a clue."

"But what if she *does*? What if she realizes her mistakes but doesn't know how to make up for them?"

Sarah sighed. "I'm not sure she realizes anything."

"Maybe not." Ruth fell into a kitchen chair, still holding Penny. "But we have to give her a chance. After that ..."

"What?" Maddy sat down opposite her.

"I don't know. Depends on what happens."

"Well, I don't think Ben will stand for it." Sarah ran a hand through her short brown hair. "You can know Jess gave him an earful. He'll come home with one thought on his mind—get rid of Edna Day."

"We can't make her leave town," Ruth said. "That's the problem."

"Is he bad tonight?" Jess's words, spoken into the phone, caught Ruth's attention. She turned toward her youngest daughter.

"Is it Henry?" Maddy called to Jess.

Henry Curd, Tamel's father, was only 66, but years of smoking and little exercise had left him with bad lungs and a worse heart.

Jess waved a hand at her. "I'm so sorry," she said into the phone. "You want me to come over?" She listened. "They don't need me here, they can deal with it." She flicked a glance toward the living room. "I think."

Maddy winced at Sarah. "Doesn't sound good."

"No, it doesn't."

33

Henry wasn't expected to last much longer. Ruth knew his slow descent had not been easy on Tamel. In the past few months Henry had lost the ability to run his funeral home—the only one in town. Tamel was trying to sell the business.

"Okay." Jess sounded reluctant. "But call me if you need me, all right?"

She clicked off the phone and rose from the chair.

"What's goin' on, Jess?" Ruth bent over to put Penny on the floor. The Yorkie pranced across the family room to her yellow bed and flounced down on it.

Jess eased into a chair at the kitchen table. "Henry had some heart pains—well, more than usual. Tamel wanted to take him to the hospital, but he refused. Stubborn old man." She sighed. "They may still go in tonight if it gets any worse."

"Tamel doesn't want you to come?" Maddy asked.

"You know Tamel. Says he'd give me the world, but when it comes to his dad he backs off like he doesn't want me involved."

Ruth nodded. "I think he's a little ashamed, don't you? Henry wasn't all that great of a dad after his wife died. And Tamel knows we know it. We sure fed him enough times when he was growin' up."

"So what's Tamel got to be ashamed of?" Jess retorted. "*He* didn't do anything."

Ruth gave her a sad smile. For being an attorney—and arguing like one—sometimes Jess saw only what she wanted to see. "Because Henry is family. If one person in your family doesn't act right, everybody feels the shame."

Like Christina was feeling right now.

The glances around the table said they all shared the same thought.

Ruth cocked an ear toward the living room. What was going on in there? She breathed a prayer that Christina would find the right words to say.

CHAPTER 6

Christina and her mother eyed each other, both waiting for the other to speak first. Christina felt fluttery inside.

"Well. I might as well sit down." Her mother chose a chair from the shower circle and angled it toward the couch. She smacked her palms against her legs. "So. Here I am. Go ahead, lay it on me. What's so bad about my bein' here?"

As if her mother had to ask the question. Christina dropped her gaze to the carpet. How to even begin? How do you cover a lifetime of abuse in one conversation?

Her mother huffed a sigh. "At least tell me why you told my evil sister you were gettin' married when you wouldn't even let *me* know."

Christina shook her head. "I didn't tell her. I don't know how she found out. Some friend of a friend, I guess."

"Oh. So you didn't want *anyone* in your terrible family to know. Now that you're gettin' a new one and all."

"I fell in love with Ben, Mom. It's not my fault he comes from a loving family."

Edna drew back her head. "And yours wasn't?"

Christina shot her an incredulous look.

"Your dad provided for you, didn't he? Put food on the table."

Righteous anger bristled through Christina. "Barely! Half the time he was drunk. And a lot of the time when there *was* food on the table, *I* couldn't eat it, because I was locked in the closet."

Her mother pushed air through her lips. "He only did that once or twice."

"Like that would be okay? And it wasn't once or twice. It was over and over, month after month, year after year!" The memories kicked up a dust storm in Christina.

"Well, I sure don't know where *I* was."

Christina gripped the sofa cushions. "You were right there, letting him!" She was so *sick* of her mother's denials. "And that's your rationalization, isn't it? You never hit me yourself. *You* never locked me in the closet. You didn't have to. *He* did it for you! And you *let* him!"

Her mother stared at her, mouth open.

"How *could* you? What did I ever do to you?"

Edna Day shifted in her seat, her gaze rising above Christina's head. "I couldn't stop him." Her voice was low. "He shoved me around too, you know. What do you think he'd a done to me if I stood in his way?"

"So you saved yourself over your *child*? You could have acted like a *mother*."

Edna lowered her eyes to Christina. Was there a glint of moisture there?

Well, too little, too late. Christina couldn't stand how her mother always explained everything away, how she

38

refused to take responsibility for the suffering she'd caused. "Besides, I never saw *any* hint on your face that you cared what happened to me."

Her mother swallowed. A tear fell on her cheek. It was the first time Christina had ever seen her cry.

"But I'm here now." Edna raised a hand and let it fall back into her lap. "Doesn't that tell you somethin'?"

Christina watched the tear track down her mother's worn face, and — amazingly — her anger faded. Tiredness crept in behind it. What more could she say now, with the Dearings nearby and Ben about to arrive home any minute? The subject was too big, too bulging with pain. For the past few months she'd been going to church with Ben. Growing closer to God, asking Him to help her get over her past. Christina wanted to let herself go and love completely, like Ben deserved. She wanted to leave her childhood and all its baggage behind, build her new life. Refuse to live like a victim. But it wasn't easy.

"*Doesn't* it, Christina?"

She put a hand to her forehead. If only she could run away and hide. "Yes, Mom, it tells me a lot. That you still think of no one but yourself."

Edna pulled back her head in shock. "What's *wrong* with a mother wantin' to be at her own daughter's weddin'?"

"You knew I hadn't invited you."

"I figured you just forgot or somethin'."

Uh-huh.

"I knew once you saw me and we could talk, you'd want me here."

More rationalizing. More lying to herself.

The day Christina turned eighteen she'd left home. She moved to Dallas and didn't tell her parents where she lived or worked. Christina never saw her father again before he died. Hadn't seen her mother since the funeral.

39

The few talks they'd had on the phone had been one-sided—her mother chattering on about all the new men in her life. Even those infrequent calls Christina had made were out of some weird sense of duty. Her tone of voice had said as much.

"Christina, *I* didn't do all those horrible things to you. It was your dad. He was a bad one."

This was useless.

"Why'd you marry him, then?"

"I loved him."

"You couldn't tell he was abusive? And a drunk?"

Her mother shrugged. "That's the way men are."

Christina pictured Ben. His father and two brothers-in-law. "Not all of them. Not most of them, in fact."

Her mother scratched her neck. "Guess I just couldn't pick men right."

"Guess not."

They looked away from each other. Silence swirled and tugged.

What were Mama Ruth and her three daughters saying in the kitchen? Surely they thought less of Christina after seeing her mother for themselves. They had to be sorry Ben was marrying into such a messed up family.

"You don't really want me to go home, do you?" Edna lifted her chin. Under one eye her thick mascara had smeared from the tear. She was only fifty-one, but she looked ancient. Hard and worn.

Christina didn't respond.

Hurt creased her mother's forehead.

Deep inside Christina a tiny seed of compassion cracked open. Where had *that* come from? Edna Day hardly deserved it. Still, it was so rare to see the slightest vulnerability on her mother's face.

40

"If you want me to leave this house right now, I will."
Christina's mother gestured with her chin toward the
kitchen. "Everybody in your new *family* will sure be glad.
All those women at your shower, too. They'll all crowd
around you at the weddin' and say what a sorry wreck
your mama is. Somethin' the cat drug in."

"No they won't."

"Yes they will. I saw their faces."

Another tear fell on Edna's cheek. She sniffed. "I
don't want them to hate me. I don't want *you* to hate me."

If only she could. If only it were that simple. "I don't
hate you."

Her mother peered at her. "You act like you do. Not
invitin' me to your weddin'."

Christina sighed. "Maybe I'm just not strong enough
yet to handle being around you."

"What's that supposed to mean?"

Christina rubbed one thumb over the other. Back and
forth, back and forth. "I don't trust you."

Her mother's mouth slacked. "Why not?"

Christina shook her head. Two spinning balls, that's
what they were. Going 'round and 'round. Why had she
even brought up the word *trust*? She'd had to deal with
that topic far too much in therapy. Last summer her lack
of trust had almost cost Christina her engagement to Ben.
It continually wanted to derail her life. She had to *fight* for
the ability to trust.

Impatience tinged Edna's voice. "If you're still
thinkin' how your dad treated you, he's gone now."

Christina forced herself to look her mother in the eye.
"And what did *you* do? I never knew when you'd be sober
or dead drunk. And when did you ever build me up
instead of tear me down? When did you ever say 'I'm
proud of you?' Or 'I love you?'"

"I always loved you!"

41

Christina winced.

"Well, I …" Edna laced and unlaced her fingers. Emotions rippled across her face, as if she saw the truth but couldn't bear it. She raked a hand through her gaudy red hair. "I mean … I want to show it now, Christina. Really, I do."

By ruining her wedding?

"I wanna *be* here and be a mama to you. Meet the man you're gonna marry. I wanna see you happy." Edna turned away, her eyes taking on a far-off expression. For a long moment they sat in silence. When she spoke again it was almost under her breath. "I was happy once."

Christina watched her warily. Was this some new form of manipulation? But her mother had never pretended weakness or sorrow to get her way. She'd always just demanded it.

"Don't worry, Mom. I'm very happy."

Her mother absorbed the words, then nodded.

More silence, brimming with memories of taunts, tears, and betrayal. So many things Christina wanted to say. So many things she deserved to know.

She pulled a pillow onto her lap. Picked at the fabric.

From the house's west wing came the unmistakable grind of a garage door going up. Ben was home.

Christina tensed. She wasn't ready for Ben to be in the same room with her mother. He'd made it clear he couldn't stand her.

Edna looked toward the sound. "That your man comin'?"

Christina could barely nod.

Her mother pasted on a crooked smile. "Finally I get to meet him."

"Be nice. *Please.*"

"Why wouldn't I?"

The palms of Christina's hands started to sweat.

Now what?

No matter what her mother claimed, she wouldn't leave the Dearings' house easily, even if Ben told her to. He'd have to force her, and things would get ugly. Those tears would fast turn into cussing and screaming—until he'd have to call the police. They'd haul Edna Day away, maybe keep her overnight in jail. Then they'd have to let her out. At which point she'd come back, madder than ever. Christina had seen it all too often with her dad, when he'd been locked in jail for public drunkenness. Oh, when he got home. How much *worse* it had been for her.

A chill shook her limbs.

She had to stop something like that from happening. She couldn't stand to see fighting in this peaceful home, involving her Ben. She'd never heard him so much as raise his voice to anyone. And there was the whole Dearing family to think of. How could she bring such awfulness into their lives?

Jesus, help.

More grinding from the garage. The door going down.

In the core of Christina a gear slipped into place. A tiny, battered gear gritty enough to drive machinery much bigger than itself.

Muffled voices sounded in the kitchen, including Ben's. Christina made out one sentence. "Where are they?"

She threw aside the pillow and pushed to her feet.

43

CHAPTER 7

Ben headed for the living room, heart in his throat. How many times had he imagined coming face to face with Edna Day? Throwing all the words at her that she deserved—and that her own daughter would never say. But here? *Now*?

"I'll just tell her to leave," Ben's father had said on the way home. "I'm not goin' to allow any craziness in my house."

"No, Dad, I got this. I'm the one who needs to stand up for Christina."

And that's what Ben would do. He'd get her poor excuse for a mother out of the house—fast.

Ben rounded the corner and took in the scene in an instant. Presents displayed on a table—gifts from their registry that Christina should now be showing him with joy. Instead she stood facing him, every muscle locked up.

Her mother rose from a chair. Everything about her made him want to shudder—from the plunging, see-through sweater to the heavy makeup and garish hair.

From where he stood, Ben could smell the cigarette smoke.

"Well, hello there, Ben, nice to meet ya." She smiled wide, then raised her eyebrows at her daughter. "My, Chris, he's a looker."

"Her name is *Christina*."

Edna placed a hand on her chest. "Oh, that's right. It's Christina now. Sorry."

It had *always* been Christina.

Ben looked to his fiancée. "You okay?"

She nodded.

Ben held her gaze. Did she mean that? So often she hid her feelings. Baggage left from her childhood— packed by this woman.

"Why wouldn't she be okay?" Edna Day spread her arms. "Her mama's here now."

Ben wanted to punch her.

Christina's worried eyes flicked from her mother to him.

Ben moved to her side and put an arm around her shoulder. He focused on Edna. "You weren't invited here."

"I seem to recall that."

Christina shook her head. "Ben—"

"So you can leave now."

"I'm not goin' anywhere."

"Ben!" Christina's tone sharpened. "Wait."

She stepped away from him. Held up her hands, palms out. "I don't ... She needs to stay."

He frowned at her. "*What*? No."

"Yes." She swallowed. "See, we've ... worked it out. Agreed to some things. Right?" Christina turned to her mother.

Edna's brow creased. She stared at her daughter. "Yeah. Right."

Christina nodded again — too hard. "First of all, my mother's staying at the motel." Christina's words tumbled from her. Was that perspiration on her forehead? "And she promises she won't drink. Because she knows if she gets drunk that's just ... not going to work here. Right, Mom?"

Edna's lip curled. Then flattened. "Yeah, sure." She waved a hand in the air. "Who needs alcohol? It's only for a couple days."

Christina's cheeks flushed. "And she has her own car so—"

"Hey, Christina." Her mother stuck out a hip. "I can talk for myself, you know."

Christina's expression mixed pleading and fear. "Sorry."

"No way, you do *not* have to be sorry for anything." Ben turned to Edna. "You need to go. *Now.*"

Her face hardened. "Why?"

As if she had to ask. As if this woman had done anything, any *single* thing, to earn the right to be at her daughter's wedding.

"Because Christina doesn't want you here."

Edna's mouth turned down. "That's not what I heard."

"You don't *see* her. You don't see anyone but yourself."

Christina's eyes closed. "Ben, please ..."

"How *dare* you talk to me like that?" Edna flexed her jaw. "How long have you known my daughter, a few months? I spent eighteen years with her."

"Eighteen *miserable* years."

"Ben," Christina said, "I want her here."

"No you don't."

"Yes I do."

47

"See?" Edna folded triumphant arms. "You're no different than the rest of your family. Every one of y'all act like I'm not good enough for you."

"That's because you're not. And you're not one *tenth* of what your daughter is, no matter—"

"You can't *talk* to me like that!"

Ben pointed at her. "This is my parents' house. I grew up here. And as long as you're in it, you're gonna hear what I have to say."

Christina was crying. He gripped her arm.

"Well, I don't want to be in your fancy house anyway." Edna Day wagged her head. "Like Chris— *Christina*—said, I'm stayin' at the motel. I don't have to be anywhere near the likes of you." Edna's voice wavered. "But I *am* seein' my daughter get married, no matter what you say. I got a right to do that." Edna stepped back and ran a hand across her face. "After that I'll just get my miserable self on home."

Christina sniffed. "Mom, you don't have to go."

Ben stared at his fiancée. Since when did she defend her mother? And against *him*?

Fear trickled through his veins. The last time Christina was here in July, she'd almost broken up with him because of her past, claiming she'd never fit in with his family. So much of her was still fragile. What if she did that again?

"Look." Christina wiped a tear from her cheek. "I just don't want a fight, Ben, okay?" She turned to her mother. "Stay for the wedding. Just … please. Do what I asked."

"Fine. Deal." Edna stuck out a purple-nailed hand. "Nice to meet ya, Ben Dearing. Future son-in-law."

Ben eyed her. The stories he'd heard of this woman. The things she'd allowed Christina to endure. He didn't want to so much as touch Edna Day.

48

He shifted his focus to Christina. Her eyes pled with him. If he didn't go along with this would he push her away?

Ben took a deep breath and lifted his arm to shake Edna's hand. When she started to pull away he gripped harder, sending a silent, burning message. *Don't you dare hurt my Christina — or you'll have to deal with me.*

Edna narrowed her eyes.

Ben released her fingers.

Christina mouthed *Thank you.* She blinked the last of her tears away.

The three of them stood in awkward silence.

Edna placed her hands on her hips. She gazed around the room. "Well. Lots of nice gifts in here, I see."

Ben's jaw felt hard as a rock. How could this be happening?

"I, uh … I still have mine to give you. I'll bring it to the weddin'."

Christina nodded.

More silence. Ben pictured his family in the kitchen, waiting on tenterhooks for him to reappear. How was he supposed to tell them he'd let Edna stay? Jess would pitch a fit.

"Well." Edna shifted her feet. "Guess I'll be gettin' back to the motel now."

Something twinged across Christina's face. Pity? Sense of duty? She gazed at Ben. He gave his head a slight shake — *what?*

Christina flicked her eyes toward the kitchen.

Oh, no. Huh-uh. If she wanted her mother to meet the rest of the family, as if Edna was really welcome here, that was going too far.

Edna watched their wordless interchange with an expression mixing anxiety and smugness.

Ben took Christina's hand. "We're gonna go talk for a minute," he said to Edna.

She nodded, then made a point of sitting straight-backed in a chair.

Ben led Christina out of the living room and down the hall. As they passed the entrance to the family room, Jess spotted them.

"What's happenin'?" She hurried to the doorway. "She gone yet?" Her whisper was loud.

Ben felt Christina tense. "No, and keep your voice down. We gotta talk a minute."

"Why's she still—"

"Jess, stay out of it, okay?" The last thing he needed was for Christina and his sister to go at it again. Especially over someone like Edna Day.

How in the world had this weekend gotten so messed up?

Jess rolled her eyes as if to say *just trying to help.* She retreated back into the family room.

Ben pulled Christina into the guest room and shut the door. He spread his arms. "*What* is goin' on? You didn't even want to tell your mother about the weddin'. Now she's here and you don't want her to *leave?*"

Christina's face flushed. "Just let her meet everyone else. Then she can go back to the motel."

"Why? Like she'll fit in?"

"No, but—"

"And who knows what Jess will do."

Christina's mouth firmed. "Does Jess run your family?"

"Look. I don't want to fight." Ben heaved a sigh. "*Why* are you doin' this?"

Christina stared at the wall, as if searching for an answer. "Because she *won't* leave town, Ben, even if you told her to. Now that she's here we have to make the best of it. It's the only way. Maybe if we keep her fairly close, she'll stay under control and not drink. If we make her mad, no telling what she'll do." Christina rubbed her face. "So for right now, let's have her meet everyone and get it over with. Better than having her meet people at the wedding reception, with all our guests watching."

Was it? Ben's mind had been jerked this way and that, until he didn't know *what* to think. "What about tomorrow and Saturday mornin'? We've got all the rest of the family comin' in. Aunts and uncles and cousins. Not to mention the rehearsal supper tomorrow night. You want her there, too? Just hangin' around with everybody the next two days?"

"I ..." Christina's eyes flooded with new tears. She slumped onto the bed and hid her face in her hands.

Ben let his chin drop. Oh, man. If things went really south with Edna, Christina would feel even more ashamed. He couldn't bear to see that.

He sat down on the bed and pulled Christina close. "Come on now, it's okay. We'll make this work. Somehow."

Christina's body shook with sobs. "When she showed up in front of all those women, I thought I'd *die*."

"I know." Ben's heart clinched. "I'm so sorry."

"I just didn't know what to *do*. It's not fair that she came. Not fair at all."

"No. It's not."

Christina cried for a while longer, then pulled in a long breath. "Okay. I need to ..." She straightened. "We have to go back out there. Let's just ... do this fast and get her out of here. I don't know about tomorrow. I can't even think about that right now."

Ben patted his fiancée on the shoulder. "You're bein' amazingly strong. If you really want to do this, we will. Together."

51

Christina nodded. She wiped the remaining tears from her face and stood. Held out her hand. "I love you, Ben Dearing."

He rose and wrapped her in his arms. "I love you too. So much."

Enough, even, to subject his own beloved family to a woman he despised.

CHAPTER 8

Narrow-eyed, Jess leaned against a kitchen counter, watching Edna Day work her half-dressed, sandpaper-voiced way across the family room. Wasn't this just the bee's knees. One big happy family in the Dearing household.

What on *earth* had come over Ben, letting that woman stay here? And come to the *wedding*?

Christina couldn't have described her mother badly enough if she'd tried. Which she hadn't, at least not to Jess. But Ben had filled Jess's ears more than once. Hearing details of Christina's childhood had helped Jess understand her better—and goodness knows a little more understanding between the two of them was a good thing. But it had also made Jess detest the woman who'd stormed into her parents' home.

With the help of Jess's mom, Christina was leading her own mother around, introducing her to Jess's dad, Jake, and Don. All of whom, of course, declared how glad they were that Edna had come. Nothing but politeness out of those three Southern gentlemen.

And a lot of uplifted eyes as they tried not to stare at the woman's chest.

No doubt when Tamel met Edna he'd be just as sociable as the rest of the men. Drat them all. Trustworthiness in a woman like that was scarce as hen's teeth—especially when she was around the opposite sex. Jess wouldn't put anything past her.

And Christina? One thing Jess did well was read people. And that girl was one pulsing blender of emotion.

Ben eased up beside Jess, watching Christina with a hawk's eye.

"You gonna tell me what happened?" Accusation twanged her words.

"Christina insisted it's the best way to keep the peace."

"We were peaceful before she got here."

"Come on, Jess, this is hard enough. I don't need you on me. And don't you dare get on Christina."

"*Why* would I get on her?"

"Because you say whatever you think, that's why. And right now she can't take it. She's barely holdin' it together. You gotta be as supportive as you can."

"For two days. Keep my mouth shut for *two whole days* while that woman is here."

"Yeah. Exactly."

Jess made a sound in her throat. "I'm likely to kill her first."

Second time she'd said that.

This was going to be some wedding.

Across the room Christina introduced her mother to Pogey. Even from here Jess could tell his pudgy, freckled cheeks looked a little pale. All the same he stuck out his hand with a "Nice to meetcha."

"Ain't you cute." Edna pinched his cheek. It's a wonder her long nails didn't dig ditches in his face. Pogey pulled from her grasp and backed up a step.

Jess's mom gave him a grandmotherly pat.

Lady Penelope perched on her bed, ears alert. The pink bejeweled crown hanging from her collar swayed now and then as her little head followed Edna Day's every move. Every time Edna emitted one of her grating laughs, Penny growled. Sarah had gone over to hush her three times.

"And who's this little girl?" Edna leaned down close to Alex. The five-year-old made a face and drew away.

"This is Alex, Maddy and Don's daughter." Christina's voice sounded over-bright.

Alex curled in one shoulder. "Who are *you*?"

"I'm Christina's mama."

"Your breath stinks." Alex twisted her mouth.

A chortle popped out of Jess's mouth. Ben smacked her on the arm.

Edna drew back. "Oh."

Christina flashed Alex a look that mixed embarrassment and irritation.

"Now, Alex, that's not nice." Maddy swooped in and shepherded her daughter away. "So sorry," she mumbled over her shoulder to Edna.

"Don't worry 'bout it."

Sweet little six-year-old Lacey, Sarah and Jake's daughter, managed to meet Edna without making a face or snide comment. But she did find her exit as fast as possible. She headed straight for Penny's bed and sat down cross-legged beside it. Penny found her way into Lacey's lap.

"Is that the dog I heard barkin'?" Edna asked. "Such a cute little thing." She moved toward Penny. The Yorkie tried to disappear against Lacey's belly.

55

"Come on, little one." Edna's croon was as inviting as a hedgehog's hide. She held out a hand.

The Yorkie exploded into barks that shook her entire body.

"Hush, Penny!" Lacey picked her up.

Jess's mom cast Edna an apologetic look. "I'm so sorry. She usually doesn't do that."

Edna firmed her mouth. "Saved it for me, huh."

"I didn't mean —"

"No worries."

Edna tried to smile. It looked ... brittle.

Jess's cell phone rang — Tamel's ringtone. She snatched it up from the counter. "Hi, how's your dad?" She turned and walked toward the west wing for some privacy.

"He seems okay. Sleepin' for now."

She let out a long breath. "Oh. Good."

"So how's it goin' over there?"

"Fabulous. Witchy Woman's now meetin' the family so she'll feel right at home for the weddin'."

"I see." Tamel drew out the words. "What happened?"

"It's complicated."

"Yeah." Tamel spoke softly. "The parent/child thing often is."

Jess knew he spoke half for himself. "I'm sorry, Tamel. Wish I could stay in Justus longer and help you." On Sunday she had to go home, leaving Tamel once again in his dismal, small-town life, nursing his irascible father. With her hectic schedule at Dunham, Biggs, and Tooley in Memphis, Jess couldn't visit Justus all that often. And Tamel was afraid to leave his father to visit her.

"Don't worry about me," Tamel said. "I'm just sad for Christina. She must be beside herself."

"She's beside her mom, which is worse."

"Well, go easy on 'em, okay? For Ben's *and* Christina's sake."

Jess straightened her back. "Why is everybody gettin' on me, like I'm the bad guy here? Edna's the one who's crashed the party."

"But it's Christina's and Ben's party. So you gotta help make the peace."

"I'm a contracts lawyer. I do not make peace."

"You can do this, Jess. I'm countin' on you."

She pictured Tamel's mischievous smile and dimples, his brown eyes. The man sure could get under her skin. "Yeah, okay. I'll ... control myself."

"That's my girl."

Jess made a face. She *could* do this—for her brother's and Christina's sake. Right? Just stay out of the evil woman's way. Bite her own tongue. A lot. Somehow she'd get through the next two days without coming head to head with Edna Day.

Easy as falling off a greasy log.

CHAPTER 9

"See, that wasn't so bad." Syton Dearing sat on the bed and started taking off his shoes. "I think we'll get through the weekend just fine."

What a day. It was after eleven, and Ruth's head throbbed with exhaustion. Truth was, she'd been tired when the day began. All the wedding preparations and grocery shopping for all the guests coming in. Plus the shower.

A little while ago Edna had finally left for the night, and the kids were headed to bed. The two grandgirls had long since gone to sleep in the west wing play room. Pogey was on the floor of his parents' room. Ben had still looked a little shock-worn as Ruth hugged him goodnight. Christina looked worse. But both declared they were okay.

"It's not so bad as long as Christina wants her mama here." Ruth sank down next to Sy. "I just didn't know how to get Edna out of the house and be polite to her at the same time."

Sy chuckled, creasing the lines around his blue eyes. "That would call for some finessed Southern hospitality. Feed her cake and coffee, then shove her out the door."

Ruth gave him a look. "You can laugh. You weren't here, with all the women at that shower. I swear, when Edna took off her coat everyone nearly choked."

"I 'bout choked myself when I saw how she was dressed." Sy leaned back and made a point of looking Ruth up and down. "You'd look good in a sweater like that."

"Ho boy, for you maybe. I wouldn't be caught dead in such a thing outside the bedroom door."

"Behind the bedroom door would be just fine with me."

They grinned at each other.

"So what's on the calendar for tomorrow?" Sy pulled off a sock.

Men. No matter how many times you told them, they just couldn't seem to keep social dates in their head.

"Lots of things. First of all, my brother and his wife are arrivin', plus Ben's and Christina's two friends. Your side of the family arrives late tomorrow night, so we'll just see them at the weddin'. I'll probably need you to do an airport run after breakfast."

"Okay. Just point me to the car when it's time." Sy gave Ruth that martyred *I-just-live-here* look. He never stopped teasing her.

"I'll be feeding people as they roll in. Then there's the rehearsal at the church at four. And after that, supper for everybody here. Thank goodness at least that's catered." Ruth blew out air. "I swear I'll just collapse when this is all over."

Sy leaned over and kissed her. "You'll be great, Ruthie. No better hostess than you."

"We shall see. Already I feel like half the day will be spent keepin' certain people apart. Like Jess and Edna. And little Alex and Edna. Not to mention Penny and Edna." Ruth tilted her head. "You seein' a pattern here?"

Sy scratched his cheek. "Why do you think Christina caved in to her mom so quickly? Just afraid to say no?"

Ruth shook her head. "If it was only fear, I'd have talked her out of it. It's way more than that. Christina doesn't like or trust her mother, but she *wants* to. Know what I mean? And Edna knows her daughter doesn't want her around, but she *wants* Christina to want her. Although if she wants to have her daughter's love, you'd think she'd show a little love herself."

Sy lifted a shoulder. "Maybe she doesn't know how."

The very thought of such ignorance made Ruth shiver. "Maybe not. But I just can't imagine it."

Sy ran his finger down Ruth's nose. "If anyone can reach her, you can."

"Uh-huh. Ben told me, 'Now, Mama, don't go tryin' to be her best friend. All we gotta do is get through the weddin'.'"

"Maybe he's right. You don't want Christina thinkin' you're dividin' your loyalty."

Whoa. "Would she think that?"

"Maybe." Her husband sighed. "Women are funny creatures. Way too hard for us simple men to understand."

Ruth gave him a lopsided smile. "Don't try. Just love us."

Sy smiled back. "That's what it's all about."

CHAPTER 10

Christina opened her eyes in the guest room to early morning light filtering through the red curtains. The digital clock on the bedside table read 6:58. For an instant she thought only, *This is the day before my wedding.*

Then the memory flooded back. Her mother was here. Even worse, she was staying at the town's only motel — the same one where all the family members who were arriving today would be staying. No one had even mentioned that last night, but Christina knew it must be on everyone's mind.

It was enough to make Christina want to hide in bed all day.

She listened for sounds in the house. All was quiet. Above her were Ben's and Jess's old rooms. Nearby on the first floor were Sarah's and Maddy's. The master suite was upstairs in the west wing.

Surely Mama Ruth was up. She had an awful lot of hostessing ahead of her today.

And she would need help.

With a sigh, Christina heaved herself from bed.

Sitting on the edge of the mattress, she prayed for some serious divine intervention. That God would help her mother get along with everyone. That Edna Day wouldn't drink. That she wouldn't totally spoil the rehearsal supper tonight. Or, please God, the wedding.

Had she done the right thing in letting her mother stay?

Putting on makeup, brushing her long blonde hair, Christina tossed answers to the question back and forth in her mind. Yes, she had. No, she hadn't. Everything would be okay. Everything would be a disaster. This would be the worst wedding ever.

If something terrible did happen, she would never forgive herself for ruining the day.

Christina slipped down the hall and into the family room. Penny came trotting out of her bed.

"Hello, Lady P." She bent over and picked up the Yorkie. Penny nestled up and gave her a doggy smile. Christina scratched behind her ears. "You didn't like my mother, did you."

Penny wagged her little tail.

"That's okay. I don't like her much either."

Mama Ruth came into the kitchen from the west wing hall. "Good mornin'!"

"Morning." Christina put Penny down.

Mama Ruth walked over to give Christina a hug. She wore no makeup yet but was still pretty, with her smooth skin and short chestnut hair. She stood only five-two, way shorter than anyone else in the family. But she had energy and love enough to match all of them.

Mama Ruth stood back and gazed at Christina. "How are you?"

"Okay."

"Really?"

"Yeah." Christina tried to smile.

Mama Ruth placed her hands on Christina's shoulders. "Know what? I think your mama very much wants to make this work. She wants to prove she can be a part of your new family."

Of course she wanted to prove that. In the end, it was still all about Edna Day, wasn't it? "I guess."

Mama Ruth gave Christina another long look, then turned back to the kitchen. She took a huge rectangular pan of food off the counter and slid it into the oven. Set the timer. "This breakfast casserole will take about half an hour to bake on convection. We'll have toast too, from some of that bread I made earlier this week."

One of the many things Mama Ruth did well—feed her family.

"I've got coffee goin', but I suppose you and Sarah will want to do your own thing."

Christina smiled. At the family reunion, Sarah had won Christina over to her strong, creamy lattes. "Yeah. I'll wait for Sarah." Christina looked around the kitchen. "Something I can do?"

"No, no. The girls will help me later. Right now I'd just enjoy the quiet if I were you. Won't last long."

Sure didn't. Within half an hour the whole family was up, crowding around the breakfast table, making toast and drinking coffee. Sarah was working her magic on the espresso machine. Ben stuck close to Christina, as if not sure whether she could hold it together. Three times he asked if she was all right.

"Ben," she finally told him, "chill out. You think this is gonna do me in, after all I've been through?"

Inside, she didn't feel half so sure of herself.

He gazed at her. "Just checkin'."

65

"How's Tamel's dad this mornin', Jess?" Mama Ruth asked.

Jess looked great, as she always did. She was tall with vivid green eyes. The only girl in the family who bleached her hair blonde. It skimmed her shoulders in a blunt, stylish cut. Christina knew Jess started most days by running four miles. She'd probably already been out this morning.

"Sounds like he's a little better." Jess reached for a coffee mug. "Good thing. Tamel needs to be at the rehearsal this afternoon. I'm gonna go check on 'em both after breakfast."

The family seemed to be avoiding the subject of Christina's mother, bantering with each other as usual. Don and Jake were digging at Ben about his wedding and how the rest of his existence would be "spent in servitude."

"Where's that 'My Life is Over' T-shirt you brought, Don?" Jake pushed up his wire rim glasses. One side of his jet black hair stuck out, bedhead style. Sarah wet her hand and tried to smooth the hair down.

"In the room." Don gestured with his chin toward the east wing. "I'm givin' it to Ben soon as he says 'I do.' He can wear it on the honeymoon."

Christina looked to Ben—*would he do that?* Ben shook his head. Christina concentrated on her plate. She still didn't always get this family's teasing.

"I'll take another piece of that dy-no-mite toast." Syton Dearing sat in his chair at the head of the long kitchen table. "I'll need fuel to get through this crazy day."

Maddy jumped up. "I'll make your toast for you, Daddy." She cut a thick slice off the loaf and dropped it into the toaster.

Christina took a bite of casserole. Sausage and eggs, with a kick to it. Tasted wonderful.

Her mind wandered to her mother. What was she doing right now? Still sleeping? Had she been up late last night, hitting the bars? Not that there were many places to go drinking in Justus. But she only needed one. The thought of her mother running around town today made Christina's stomach clench. No telling what she'd get herself into.

For a moment the kitchen fell quiet. Christina glanced at the kids in the adjoining family room. Alex, Lacey, and Pogey were watching TV with the sound turned low. Sarah, Pogey's mom, had made him put shoes on. As usual his feet were smelling up the house. Penny lay on Lacey's lap. "I wish Ben got married every weekend," Alex said. "So we could get out of more school."

Lacey lifted a shoulder. "I like school. Maybe you'll like it better when you're in first grade. Kindergarten is kinda borin'."

"It is not!" Alex couldn't stand for anybody to talk down any part of her life.

"I didn't mean—"

"It is *not* borin'."

"Okay, okay, it's not." Lacey flicked a look at the ceiling with all the wisdom of an extra year's experience in life. "Sheesh."

"Will you two be quiet!" Pogey edged closer to the TV. He wore a frown that wouldn't quit. "I can't hear."

"It's a stupid show anyway." Alex crossed her arms.

Christina couldn't see what they were watching.

"It's not stupid, it's above your head."

"What's above my head?" Alex looked up.

Pogey held up both hands in frustration. "I mean it's smarter than you are. Too s'phisticated."

"Pogey." Jake shook a finger at his son. "Don't go baitin' your cousin like that."

"I'm not baitin' her." Pogey sounded downright ticked off, unusual for him. He was typically a pretty mild kid.

Jess gave him a look. "What's the matter with you, Pogey?"

"Nothin'." His shoulders hunched.

"Doesn't look like nothin' to me."

"Well, it feels like it to *me*." Pogey hunched more.

"Oooh." Jess widened her eyes. "What's this from the ten-year-old, a bit of sarcasm? That's my job, Pogey."

Sarah leaned toward her sister. "He's poutin' 'cause he's got to be in the weddin' tomorrow."

Christina's mouth opened. First she'd heard of this. The two little girls had begged to be in it, and she hadn't wanted to leave Pogey out.

"Aw." Ben pushed back his chair. "Pogey, you don't wanna be in your favorite uncle's weddin'?"

Pogey shrugged.

"Wait a minute, I thought *I* was his favorite uncle." Don put on a peeved look.

Ben waved a hand. "You married into the family, you don't count."

"Hey!" Maddy huffed.

"Pogey!" Ben leaned back, getting a clean line of sight on his nephew. "Talk to me, boy."

Pogey shook his head.

"Do I have to come over there and turn you upside down?"

Pogey jerked around to look Ben in the eye. "Fine then. I don't wanna wear a monkey suit."

Ben shot Christina an amused look. She didn't see the humor. First her mother showed up, and now her nephew-to-be didn't want to be in the wedding? This weekend was getting worse by the minute.

"We're all wearin' monkey suits," Ben said. "Me, Tamel, your two other uncles, and your dad. Grandpa too, even though he's not in the weddin'."

"Yeah." Sy nodded. "I didn't want to feel left out."

"And all the women will be real dressed up." Sarah smiled at Christina. "Wait till you see Christina's dress."

"I want to see her dress." Ben looked hopeful.

"I wasn't talkin' to you."

Ben turned his attention back to Pogey. "You get to carry the ring. That's an important job. If I don't get that ring on Christina's finger, she won't really be married to me. And it'll be all your fault."

"Oh, way to go, little brother." Maddy wagged her head. "Put the guilt of a whole marriage on a ten-year-old."

"Pogey." Christina spoke up. "You don't have to be in the wedding if you don't want." Pogey was a good kid. He'd won her heart last summer when he played the piano and sang in a sweet voice that set Penny to howling—a primal doggie act far beneath her dignity.

Ben raised his eyebrows. "What? Of course he does."

"Well, not if he doesn't—"

"He wants to. Right, Pogey? Don't you wanna make Christina happy?"

"No, Ben." Christina caught his arm. "Don't put that on him. It's okay."

Alex poked Pogey in the shoulder. "*I* don't care if you're not in the weddin'."

He glared at the TV.

Ben gave his niece a look. "Way to go, Alex. Pogey, there's cake at the weddin'."

Pogey straightened with a sigh. "No, there's not. It's at the reception. I know a thing or two 'bout weddin's."

"Oh, do you now."

Sarah and Jake looked at each other questioningly, then shrugged.

"Yeah." Pogey turned to face Ben. "I've seen 'em on TV. Somethin' always goes wrong. Always. And I don't want anything goin' wrong in this family." He looked at the floor. "It's the only one I got."

A chill crept over Christina. For sure this was about her mother. Pogey was a sensitive kid. He must have felt the tension last night more than he let on.

Ben slid his arm around her, as if he knew what she was thinking. "Don't," he whispered.

Sarah rose from the table and walked over to her son. "Pogey. Nothin's gonna happen to this family. TV's full of drama, that's what it's for."

He gazed up with an almost plaintive expression, then nodded.

Ruth and Syton exchanged a look. Sy wrinkled his nose at her, and she smiled back. A worried smile.

Sarah ruffled Pogey's short hair, then straightened. "Okay, kids, TV's goin' off. Y'all need to eat some breakfast."

Lacey put Penny on the carpet and turned off the TV. The Yorkie trotted to her bed.

Christina's throat felt tight. Her mother wasn't even here, and look at how she was affecting everyone. It would be like this—likely worse—all day. And tomorrow. She never should have caved into her mother so quickly. She should have tried ... something. Anything.

Christina pushed her chair back from the table. Ben laid his hand on her arm. "You don't have to get up."

She shook her head. "The kids need room to eat. I'm done anyway." Wayward tears bit her eyes, and she fiercely blinked them back. She would not cry in front of the family. It would only make them feel worse. She stood up. "Pogey, come on, sit here."

He wandered over. Christina patted his shoulder. "You really don't have to be in the wedding if you don't want. Someone else can just hold the rings until we need them."

Pogey locked eyes with her, his tongue pushing out his top lip. A concerned expression crossed his freckled face, as if he'd noticed the remaining glint of tears in her eyes. Christina couldn't bear for him to think he'd caused them. She smiled brightly. "Okay?"

He nodded. "Know what though?" He spoke with all the wisdom he could muster. "It's prob'ly a good thing."

"Really?"

"Yeah. 'Cause I don't think anyone can take care of the rings as good as I can."

"That's it, Pogey!" Ben said.

Pogey's eyes remained on Christina. A silent message flowed between them, as if he saw through her. Which made her want to cry all the more.

She hugged him hard. "You're a great kid."

He allowed the hug, then stepped back. With a final solemn nod to her, he took his seat.

Everyone around the table seemed to draw in a cleansing breath.

Mama Ruth began clearing plates. "Sy, Keith and Dora arrive at the airport at nine-thirty."

That would be Mama Ruth's brother and his wife. Christina hadn't met them yet. She and Ben needed to do an airport run themselves in a few hours to pick up her friend, Tanya, who would be maid of honor, and Ben's friend, Jamie, his best man. They were on the same flight from Dallas.

"All right, woman, whatever you say." Syton saluted.

Mama Ruth shot him a mock frown.

"I can go for you, Sy," Don said.

71

"Yeah, let us go." Maddy touched her dad's arm. "You and Mama got enough to do."

Sy was easily swayed.

The adults rose as the kids sat down. Ben tugged Christina's hair. "I'll be right back." He headed for his bedroom.

She began picking up plates. Mama Ruth laid a hand on top of hers. "No, Christina, not the day before your weddin'. I have plenty of helpers here."

Christina hesitated, then nodded.

Unsure of what to do next, she wandered into the family room. Lady Penelope left her royal bed to greet her, as if to say *I know you're upset. It's okay.* Christina picked her up. "You are the best dog ever."

Penny gazed back. *Of course I am.*

Yorkie in her arms, Christina walked toward the guest room. When she was in the hall the kitchen phone rang. She heard Mama Ruth answer.

"Oh, hello, Dana."

The police chief's wife. Christina slowed.

"Thank you for callin'. Yes, we're fine today."

Christina listened to the clatter of plates.

"No." Ruth's voice edged. "What happened?"

Christina froze. A forever minute ticked by.

"Oh, dear. I'm sorry she's caused Buddy trouble."

Buddy. The police chief?

"Well, I know it's not, but ..."

All other sounds from the kitchen stopped.

"We'll try to find her and have a talk with her."

Oh, no. What had her mother done?

"Yes. All right. Thank you for callin'."

A drawn out silence. Christina still couldn't move.

"What happened, Mama?" Jess's voice.

Brittle-hearted, Christina turned back toward the kitchen.

CHAPTER 11

Jess drew her jacket around herself as she stomped down the front porch steps. Still chilly out. She'd even worn running gloves this morning on her jog.

She twisted her mouth as she started the car, the tirade she planned to give Edna Day running through her head.

Nine o'clock, and already the woman was causing a ruckus. Actually, she hadn't even waited till morning. According to Dana Altweather, she'd started last night. She had not gone straight to the motel after leaving the house. Oh, no, that would be far too civil. Instead she'd stopped in at Tooley's Bar for "just a little somethin'." At least that's what she claimed to the owner, Zack, as she slid onto a stool. Zack just happened to be a cousin of Buddy Altweather. That was the thing about small towns—everybody was related to everybody else, and those who weren't were neighbors. Not to mention gossips.

For all Jess knew, Edna Day's reputation had preceded her before she even entered the bar.

"Jess, *where* are you goin'?" Ben had asked as she swept up her purse after Dana's phone call. Christina stood beside him, looking pale.

"To see Tamel."

Ben drilled her a silent message with his eyes. *Don't you dare do what I know you're gonna do.*

Like anyone could stop her. She was all over this like white on rice—before Cruella Distill drank up all the liquor in Justus and ruined Ben's wedding. And likely killed a puppy or two along the way.

Jess reached the downtown area—and on impulse turned right onto Grant Street. She pulled up to Mocha Ritaville, the freestanding coffee hut owned by Rita Betts, Jimmy Buffet's most loyal fan. Not that Jess needed any more coffee. What she did need was information, and Rita was the biggest talker in town.

Rita peered out the serving window. From inside the hut drifted the sound of a Jimmy Buffet song. Jess swore the woman would play those tunes at her own funeral.

Rita's eyes lit up. "Well, just who I wanted to see, Jess Dearing."

She knew something, all right.

In early November Rita had turned 60. And had made sure the whole town knew it by sporting a "Sixty is Sexy" button pinned to her shirt for a number of weeks. Apparently she'd now switched to her Christmas mode. Rita's gray dreadlocks were wound in green and red beads. Long silver earrings dangling scarlet-nosed Rudolphs hung to her shoulders, and a garish laughing Santa fuzzed the front of her green sweatshirt. For some reason the daily lineup of jangling bracelets on her right arm were blue and orange. Apparently she didn't want to overdo the holiday thing. And her thick eye shadow? Purple, as usual. Rita Betts was a walking crayon box.

"Hi, Rita. I'll just take a small black coffee."

"Comin' right up." Rita tapped a long pink nail against the window ledge. "How y'all holdin' up over at the Dearin' House?"

Jess had always thought Rita's smoky voice was bad—until she heard Edna Day's.

"Great. Then Christina's mother showed up."

"Yeah, thought so." Rita shook her head. "That woman is *somethin' else*. She came by here yesterday, you know."

"Oh?"

"Apparently she'd just hit town and couldn't find the motel. Told me her life story. Bad little daughter didn't invite her to the weddin', and she was fixin' to go the shower."

Jess frowned. The shower hadn't started until six-thirty. Rita closed her coffee hut at five. "What time was that?"

"Just before I went home." Rita pulled down the corners of her bright red lips. "I know a troublemaker when I see one. And that gal's trouble."

"So ... you told her where the motel is? Do you think she went straight there?"

Rita emitted a throaty laugh. "Doubt it. She wanted to know if there was a bar in town. And where y'all lived. I didn't tell her 'bout neither one. First of all, the woman looked sorry enough without drinkin'. Second, I figured if Ben's pretty little gal didn't invite her own mama to the weddin' she had a mighty good reason. Besides, that reason was standin' in front a me. So I told her I didn't know where either of the places was."

"I'll bet that went over well."

75

"Like tea into Boston harbor. She cussed at me like a sailor. Said her daughter musta turned the whole town against her already. I slammed my window shut—and that was that. Didn't step outta this place until I heard her leave."

Jess's gaze drifted to the Mocha Ritaville sign. Edna Day had shown up at the shower around seven forty-five—almost three hours after talking to Rita. It couldn't have taken her that long to find the motel and ask someone how to get to the Dearing house.

Sure as shootin' she'd *planned* that late entrance.

"I heard she wrecked the shower," Rita said.

Which meant everyone in town knew by now.

"She brought it to a swift halt, that's for sure."

Rita shook her head again, sending the Rudolphs swinging. "As if that wasn't enough, she hit Tooley's afterwards."

"Yeah?"

"Filled Zack's ears up as much as she downed the whiskey. He had to cut her off."

Rita worked her mouth, pretending to debate whether to say any more. Jess waited her out.

"'Course she was too drunk to get behind a wheel. You know Zack—everybody's friend. He said he'd drive her to the motel." Rita gave Jess a meaningful look.

Oh, great. "Let me guess. She liked that a little too well."

"Yup. Tol' him he could take her back—and join her in the room for 'just one more.' Plus a little extra, if you know what I mean."

Disgust rolled through Jess. Christina would be so ashamed. She wouldn't want to show her face in town— maybe not even to walk down the aisle.

"Is that when he called the police?"

76

Dana Altweather had told Jess's mom that Perry Hall, one of the town's night officers, had been summoned to Tooley's.

"Well, not quite." Rita was clearly enjoying drawing out the juiciest story she'd been handed in months. "That would be after she threw her bar stool at him."

Oh, for— "Did she hit him?"

"He ducked." Rita grinned. "And picked up the phone he keeps on that shelf behind the counter while he was at it."

Jess leaned back against the head rest. This was insane. "So why isn't she in jail?"

"Zack didn't wanna press charges. I guess he's had a drunken binge or two in his life. Said he'd overlook this one. But she's not allowed back in Tooley's."

Well. At least that was something.

"So Perry got her to her motel room, and that was that. She's prob'ly sleepin' it off as we speak." Rita let out a beleaguered sigh. "I heard all this through the first person to drive through here this mornin'. You know Tony Willis. Finally out of his cast now, and his leg's fine."

Of course Jess knew Tony. He ran the only gas station in town. Back in the summer he'd had an argument with his mama over her new young boyfriend— Tony's best friend—and stomped down her porch stairs and fell, breaking his leg.

"Anyway, Tony was all full a the story. He also told me how Edna had filled up her car at his station last night—musta been soon after she drove through here— and was goin' on about her mean daughter and the nasty Dearin' family, and how she was gonna be at that weddin' or croak. Tony wasn't a bit surprised to hear about all the trouble she got into. He's good friends with Perry Hall, you know. That's how he heard."

77

Rita took a breath. Gossip was hard work.

"Tony said Perry told Buddy all about it this mornin'. Apparently our Chief a Police had already heard about Edna Day from his wife. Dana had nothin' good to say about the woman, who apparently embarrassed her at the shower, much less what she did to Christina and Ruth and y'all. And one thing's for sure—Buddy Altweather loves his wife, big size and all, bless her heart. Nobody treats Dana badly. Needless to say Buddy wanted in the worst way to arrest Edna Day, but Zack wouldn't budge, and that was that. And here we are."

The stream of words finally stopped. Jess rubbed her neck. "I appreciate you tellin' me, Rita."

The barista squinched her hazel eyes. "No problem. So—what y'all gonna do?"

The thing about Rita was—she gossiped both ways. A great source of information, but anything Jess told her would soon be all over town, too. "I don't know. You got any ideas?"

Rita raised her palms. "Wouldn't be for me to say. I try to keep outta people's business."

She tapped fingers against her wrinkled cheek.

"But if I was you, I'd be thinkin' of a way to run her outta town."

Jess kept her expression neutral. "How would you manage that?"

Rita shrugged. "Way she's treatin' people, someone'll likely do it for ya. Either that or she'll get herself thrown in jail."

True, but only after she did something even worse. Which Christina and Ben did not need. "Well, who knows what'll happen."

Rita nodded slowly, as if pondering the situation. She pulled her head back. "So. You ready for that coffee now?"

78

"Sure."

Rita went to pour it and came back with the to-go cup. "How's that man a yours, by the way?"

Jess knew Tamel would eventually come up. Rita had flirted with him shamelessly for years, forever demanding to know when he'd marry her. No matter that she was old enough to be his mother. Tamel took it all in stride.

"He's great. Henry's not so good, though."

"I know, I know. It's a shame."

"It is." Jess took the cup from her. "You comin' to the weddin' tomorrow?"

Rita wagged her head. "Wouldn't miss it for the world. Shuttin' this place down early so I can be there."

"That's great."

"Ben's a fine young man. I'm glad he's happy. Just don't let him live too close to his mother-in-law."

The thought hit Jess like a brick. Not that Edna lived in Dallas, but she *was* in Austin, Texas. Now that she'd forced her presence on her daughter, would she keep it up? Make Ben and Christina's lives miserable? This whole thing could be a problem for much longer than just the next two days.

"I hear you." Jess placed the coffee in her car's cup holder and reached for her purse. "Listen, Rita, I really do appreciate all the information."

"Like I said, no problem. Lemme know if I can be more help."

As Jess drove away from Mocha Ritaville she could practically feel steam coming out her ears. This woman had to be stopped — now.

Turning a corner, she headed straight for the motel and a showdown with Edna Day.

CHAPTER 12

"Thanks for your help." Ruth smiled at Sarah. The kitchen sparkled once again after their breakfast clean-up. Sarah and Ruth were alone for the moment. The kids had been shooed into their play room. Christina and Ben had gone somewhere to talk. Maddy and Don were off to the airport. Sy had decided to ride into Jackson with Jake to pick up the men's tuxes. And Jess ... ho boy.

"But of course, Mama." Sarah kissed her on the cheek. "What time is the package person comin'?"

Ruth had made arrangements with a mailing service in Jackson to package up all the presents from the shower and ship them to Ben and Christina. An expensive project, but the easiest way to take care of the gifts. They'd be timed to arrive in Dallas after Ben and Christina returned from their honeymoon.

She checked the clock. "Any time now."

As soon as they could get the living room cleared out, Ruth needed to start on lunch preparations. By one o'clock her brother, Keith, and his wife, Dora, would be here. As well as Ben's and Christina's friends from Texas, Jamie and Tanya.

Normally Ruth would be loving this gathering of family. Now worry snaked through her stomach. All the more people to witness whatever scene Edna Day might cause. She'd already broken her promise to Christina not to drink. There simply was no reining that woman in. Who knew what she might do next?

Sarah studied Ruth's face. "You okay?"

Her daughter knew her all too well. "Sure."

Sarah tilted her head. "This will work out. Really. Somehow."

She didn't sound very convincing.

What was Jess doing right now? Ruth had a mind to call Tamel and see if she really was over there. But what good would that do? If Jess was there, she'd be ticked at her mother for checking up on her. If she wasn't, Tamel would feel obligated to call Jess's cell phone and talk her out of confronting Edna. And Tamel had enough to worry about at the moment.

Life could be so complicated.

Ruth leaned against the counter. "Maybe I should go over to the motel and try to talk to Edna."

"No way, Mama. She sees you as a threat."

"I'm *not* a threat."

"You are to her. You're actin' as Christina's mama when her real one isn't wanted."

Ruth closed her eyes. Such a hard situation. She wanted to protect Christina. But the natural peacemaker in her wanted to bring Christina and her mother together. Help them see the need in each other. Not only would that smooth things over for the next two days, but it could change their lives. And Ben's life. Otherwise he would forever be in the middle of this.

Sarah pointed at Ruth. "I know what you're thinkin'. And it's not goin' to happen. At least not this weekend. There's too much goin' on right now for them to make amends for twenty-three years of bad history."

"I know. It's crazy of me to think I can do anything. But I just ... so want to fix it."

"You can't fix everything, Mama."

Ruth sighed. "Well. At least I can pray."

"Yeah." Sarah smiled. "We can all do that."

CHAPTER 13

"It's all my fault. I should have told her to go when I had the chance." Christina slumped on her bed in the guest room, Ben beside her. She felt like her world had just collapsed — even more so than last night. *Why* had she ever thought she could trust her mother?

Ben slipped his arm around Christina's shoulders. "It's not your fault. It's hers, for showin' up."

"I know, but …"

"You did what you thought was best."

Christina looked at her lap. "Yeah. Well. Shows what I know."

Ben was silent.

"I could still tell her to leave." Christina heard the reticence in her own voice. "Go to the motel and talk to her. After all, she broke her promise. She *wasn't* supposed to drink."

Ben smoothed the bedcover with a finger. "Doesn't sound like you really want to do that."

"I ... don't. Yes I do. No I don't." Christina raised her hand and let it drop. "I don't *know*."

The problem hadn't changed from last night. If she really told her mother to go, Edna Day wouldn't. She'd just get mad—and act even worse.

"You *don't* want her here, Christina." Ben's voice pulsed with frustration. "We chose not to invite her, didn't we? Moved the weddin' out of Texas just to keep her away. So tell her to leave. It's time you stood up to her."

Christina laced and unlaced her fingers. Ben would never completely understand. He didn't know what it was like to grow up with alcoholic parents. The things you did for the mere sake of survival. Her childhood had never been about what *she* wanted. It was about existing on the edge of a shivering volcano, always ready to erupt.

"We've got so much happenin' today," Ben said. "My aunt and uncle comin' in, and Jamie and Tanya. The rehearsal and supper tonight. That's just too many people for this to be goin' on. Not to mention our weddin'."

"I *know* that."

"Then do the right thing."

"You don't know what the right thing is!"

"Yes I do! You just won't *do* it. So maybe I'll have to do it for you."

Christina swiveled her head toward the wall. The breakfast she'd eaten churned in her stomach. Great. Just great. Here they were one day before their wedding—fighting.

Ben sighed. "Look. You're so sure it'll make things worse if you tell her to leave. I don't think so. I think she's tryin' to convince herself you really want her here, and as long as you say it's okay, she can believe that. The more you let her get away with stuff, the more she'll push. What about when we're married? Is she gonna show up at our place and announce she's stayin' for a visit? Because she's just sure her daughter *wants* her there, no matter what you say?"

Christina closed her eyes. "She wouldn't do that."

"How do you know?"

"I just ... know."

Part of the reason her mother had come was about saving face in front of the Dearings. Edna Day wouldn't want the whole family thinking bad about her. So she'd shown up to prove them wrong.

That was a laugh.

"Maybe she won't." Ben pushed off the bed. "But she's here now. And she's wreckin' things—and a lot of the family hasn't even shown up yet. I *don't* want her ruinin' our weddin'. Or the rehearsal and supper tonight."

"She's not invited to tonight."

"She wasn't invited to your shower either! That didn't seem to stop her."

"I—" Tears stung Christina's eyes. She pressed a hand to her mouth. She was *not* going to cry again. Before long she and Ben needed to leave for the airport. Did she really want their friends to see her with red eyes? Tanya would understand—her dear, quirky friend from work who loved kids and giraffes, of all things. But Tanya had done more than her share already of listening to Christina's hurts. This was not the time. This was the time to be *happy.*

Ben sighed. "Look, I'm sorry. I don't want to make you feel bad. I just ... somethin' has to be done about this. It's ridiculous that the whole family feels pushed around by a woman who's not even supposed to be here."

The words pierced Christina. Of course Ben was right. But he still didn't *get* it. And he never would. Did he think she didn't feel the disgust his family had toward her mother? Did he think she *wanted* to be in the middle like this? Her insides felt like they were being ripped apart.

Ben sat down again. Drummed his fingers against his knees.

What if this never worked, any of it? What if Ben was right, and her mother forever haunted them? He'd soon be up to here with it. He'd leave her for sure.

Christina flashed on a scene from childhood. Her father sitting in his chair, clutching a glass of whiskey — his third of the morning. Her mother on the worn couch. Nine-year-old Christina had finally ventured out of her bedroom, looking for something to eat. Earlier, her father had walked by her room and seen her posing in front of the mirror like a bride, pretending to hold a bouquet of flowers. Hoping, *hoping* to see something in herself that was pretty. Something a boy would want someday. Her father's guffaw had told her his opinion. As she tried to ease by his chair, he pointed at her and laughed again.

"Edna, this girl's been posin' in the mirror like some beauty queen."

Christina's mother snickered.

"Well, ya ain't, Ugly Bug. Only man that'll marry you's gonna be blind. Either that, or he'll hightail it off after a month, and you'll never see him again."

Of all the hateful words her father had spouted, those were among the ones that had stuck to her the worst. Year after year they'd dug deeper into her skin, like burrowing barbs.

Maybe her father had been right all along.

Christina's throat tightened. She hung her head — and couldn't stop the tears from flowing.

"Oh, come on, babe." Ben pulled her close. "Don't do this. We'll ... figure it out."

But something weighted his voice.

Resentment?

Christina leaned against his shoulder and cried. Ben said nothing. Just patted her shoulder, in his silent way telling her he'd wait out the tears. Again. The day before their wedding. No matter what, he was there for her.

That was so like him. He could be upset with her—which he should be—and still *give*.

The thought was not new, but it shook her.

Here she was with a man who really loved her. Who wanted to be her husband. He was *here*. Her father was gone. Why should her father's voice be louder than Ben's? And even if her mother was here, why should her presence push her away from Ben? Hadn't her parents done enough damage in her past? Did she want them to destroy her future, too?

She hadn't been through months of counseling just to lose all the strength she'd gathered now.

The tears slowed. Then stopped.

Christina's nose was running. She sat up and reached for a tissue on the nightstand.

Ben gave her a grim smile. "You okay?"

A niggling of doubt wove through her. Nothing had changed. What she was about to do could still make things worse. But which was *really* worse—to let her mother walk all over her, or go down fighting?

She pushed the doubt away and managed a smile. "I'm fine."

CHAPTER 14

Jess stalked up the motel's outside stairs to the second level. She'd left her purse in the car. Number 207 housed Texas Tyrant, according to the young gal behind the reception desk. *Tracy*, her badge had read. One of the few people in town Jess didn't know.

"You heard anything from that room this mornin'?" Jess asked her.

Tracy shook her head.

Good. Edna was probably still in bed. Here's hoping it was with a hangover and a terrible headache.

Jess was about to make it worse.

She curled her fingers into a fist and pounded on the door.

Silence.

Jess pounded again.

More silence.

"Edna!" Jess banged until her hand hurt. "Open the door!"

"Whaaaaaa?" A froggy voice filtered from the room, thick with sleep.

"Open the door, or I'm gonna knock it down!"

Jess stood back, breathing hard. She massaged her hand and winced.

"Whatdya want?" The response finally came—from just the other side of the door.

"I want to talk to you!"

A long groan. "I don' wanna talk to nobody. Go 'way."

"I can get the front desk to let me in."

"Who are you? That Dearin' girl with the big mouth?"

"It's about to get bigger. I'm not leavin' till you let me in."

Edna chuckled—a low, hoarse croak. "I'll sue you, Miss Lawyer."

Sue a lawyer who didn't tend to lose? This woman was beyond stupid.

"Let me in, Edna."

"No."

"Let. Me. *In!*" Jess kicked the door.

"I'm callin' the police."

"Oh, you just do that. Wouldn't they love to hear from you, after what happened last night."

A moment ticked by.

"Wha' happened last night?" Confusion coated Edna's words.

She really didn't remember, did she? Jess stood back, hands on her hips. Was this a good thing or a bad thing?

Jess turned to gaze across the street, considering.

She faced the door again. "You drank too much at Tooley's and threw a chair at the owner, who promptly called the police. A cop had to bring you here. Without your car, which presumably is back at the bar. The bar which, by the way, you're not allowed in again. Ever." Jess was on a roll. "Not to mention Zack Tooley is cousin to the Justus police chief, who by now has heard everything and is lookin' for any reason to run you out of town."

Okay, the last bit was a little ... embellished.

No response. Jess waited for the information to sift through the woman's thick brain.

Edna cursed. "I did *not* drink too much."

Something tinged her denial. Fear?

"Uh-huh. Let me in, and I'll tell you the rest of it."

"I'm not dressed."

"And you were last night?"

"Get *outta* here, Miss Dearing DoRight! I don't believe a word you say."

"Fine. Don't. Just do us all a favor—most of all, your daughter. Spread your bat wings and fly back to Texas. Today."

A lock banged and the door jerked half open. Edna Day stood before Jess, looking madder than a wet cat. One hand gripped the door and the other thrust into her fake red hair, which stuck out all directions like a ratted cockscomb. She wore a faded blue T shirt that came down to her thighs, *Texas Firecracker* written across her big chest.

"You listen to me." Edna pointed at Jess. "I came here to see my daughter get married, and that's exactly what I'm gonna do. And *nobody*, least of all *you*, is gonna stop me."

Jess stared at her. How could this woman be so clueless? "Christina doesn't want you here."

"How do you know what she really wants? Every girl needs her mother on her weddin' day." Edna wagged her finger. "You think you're so tough. You had it easy, girlie. You got *no idea* what my life has been. People like you

93

don't scare me. I knew y'all didn't want me here before I ever set foot in town. Did that stop me? I came here for Christina, not for you."

"She *doesn't* want you here."

"Really? Then why hasn't she said so? She had her chance last night."

"Because you sideswiped her—on purpose. She didn't know *what* to do."

Edna's lips spread in a sickening smile. "How do you know? You were huddlin' with the rest of your family in the kitchen, plannin' my hasty exit." She grated out a laugh. "And it's just drivin' you crazy, isn't it, not understandin' what happened. Not bein' able to get your hifalutin' way. Thing is, Miss Know-It-All, you ain't as smart about life as you think."

Jess stared at Edna in sheer disbelief. This woman's skull had to be five feet thick. "I'm tellin' you for the last time Christina doesn't want you here. You should have seen her face when she heard what you did last night. You promised her you wouldn't drink—and you did. You broke your end of the bargain. So *leave!*"

Edna folded her arms. "Can't you hear? I ain't goin'. Only way I would is if Christina told me to, and she ain't gonna do that. Just shows she loves her ol' mom way more than some uppity, snot-nosed new one."

Jess's arm jerked up, hand fisted. Nobody talked about her mother like that.

"Go ahead, hit me." Edna smirked. "See how fast I call the cops." She opened the door wider and spread her hands. "Here I am. Do. Your. Thing."

Jess's nerves twanged. How the woman deserved it. But that would be all she needed to play the victim. Scenes of the police arriving, mouths wagging all over town flashed through Jess's mind. Christina and Ben would be even more mortified.

She couldn't do that to them.

With purpose she relaxed her fingers. Heaved a long sigh. "Edna Day." Her words sagged with the weariness of a judge who's seen the same face one time too many in court. "It's really not smart to try to outwit me. I see right through your little tricks. You want to stay in town and take your chances—not only with the police, but with your *daughter*, go right ahead. You've trapped Christina, like you did for years when she was growin' up. Now she's desperately tryin' to keep the peace the best way she can, because she's *scared to death* of what you might do."

The defiant expression on Edna's face wavered.

"Is that what you want, Edna? To bully your daughter—*again*—after all the years of abuse? And at her *weddin'*? When she's tryin' to build the family you nev—"

"You don't know what you're *talkin'* about!" Rage reddened Edna's cheeks. "*Get out!*" She shoved the door, hitting Jess's foot.

Pain shot through Jess's toes. She jerked back.

The door slammed shut. Its lock hammered into place.

Owwww. Jess lifted her throbbing foot, steadying herself against the wall.

Something hard hit the other side of the door.

Jess made a face. She hoped it was Edna's head. And that the stupid woman broke it.

Inhaling long breaths, Jess stork-stood for another minute, trying to calm herself. Which wasn't working. Her toes screamed.

When she finally limped down the motel stairs to head for Tamel's house, she couldn't quite decide who'd won the battle.

CHAPTER 15

Tamel Curd sat forward in his father's worn armchair, a hand cupping his chin. Tiredness wound through his limbs. The night had been long. Four times he'd had to get up and tend to his dad, who'd been too weak to make it to the bathroom or raise a glass to his lips.

No way to deny it—his father wouldn't last much longer.

Emotions banged through Tamel. Sorrow. Regret. Even a tinge of relief to think it might soon be over, which led to more than a little guilt. When his father was gone, Tamel could finally return to his law career. Leave Justus and focus again on his own life. But what a price to pay. Henry Curd hadn't changed at all as his death drew near. One loving word from him, and Tamel would cling to it for the rest of his life.

Didn't look like that was going to happen.

And even after his father's passing, Tamel's work in Justus wouldn't be done. He needed to sell the funeral home and the house. Tie up all the loose ends. A thousand details to take care of.

Tamel's cell phone rang. Wearily, he checked the ID. *Lois Stanton.* A retired nurse in town who'd stayed with Tamel's father when needed. Tamel tapped the phone.

"Hi, Lois. Thanks for callin' back."

"Hello, Tamel." Her warm voice pulsed with concern. "How is he this mornin'?"

Tamel told her.

"Is he eatin' anything? Drinkin'?"

"I got a little breakfast down him. And some water."

"Good, good. Well, you know, that ol' heart is just tirin' out. But as long as he's still gettin' things down, that's a good sign."

"Yeah." Tamel took a long breath. He'd so looked forward to this weekend, with Jess in town for the wedding. But right now he just wanted a nap.

"So you need me around three-forty-five today?"

"Yes. Thanks so much. I'll try to be home from the rehearsal supper by eight. Nine at the latest."

"Don't you worry, take all the time you need." Lois hesitated. "Things … okay at the Dearin' house?"

No doubt she'd heard the news about Edna Day's arrival. Tamel didn't want to get into that. "Think so."

"Well. Good. After last night, I was worried."

Last night, meaning Edna at the shower? Or had something else happened?

Come to think of it, why hadn't he heard from Jess this morning?

"I'm sure it will all be fine. Thanks again, Lois. See you this afternoon." He hoped that didn't sound too curt.

"All righty, see ya then."

Tamel ended the call and went to his "favorites" to phone Jess. His finger was hovering over her name when the doorbell rang.

CHAPTER 16

"Goodness, that's a lot of weddin' gifts!" Martha Lou, from the shipping service, gazed at the large table in the living room, hands on her hips.

"I know." Ruth couldn't help listening for any sign of Ben and Christina. They'd gone into the guest bedroom some time ago to talk—and hadn't emerged since.

Sarah smiled. "Mama's friends were very generous."

"Well, I'll get to it." Martha Lou headed for the biggest box first. Fortunately she'd driven a large van.

Ruth stacked two boxes. "I'll help you load them."

"You don't have to do that. It's what you're payin' me for."

"Oh, no problem."

Sarah opened the front door, then returned to pick up her own load of presents. Cold air filtered into the house.

Lady Penelope trotted out of the family room to see what was happening in her domain. She sat regally in the entryway, looking from the door to Ruth as if to say, *Hey, what idiot left this open?* She gave a little doggie sneeze, her

99

topknot jerking. Then she daintily walked out to the porch and down the steps to sniff the grass.

After Ruth's second trip to Martha Lou's car, she went into the kitchen to yell down the west wing hall. "Pogey! We need your help!"

Sarah's son came out of the play room in sock feet. The smell hit Ruth before he even entered the kitchen.

"Ho, boy, go put your shoes on." She waved a hand in front of her nose.

Pogey turned around, heaving a massive sigh. No doubt he was tired of hearing from the grownups about his smelly feet. Well, they were tired of smelling them. At least the fumes were only half as bad as they were in summer.

With four people helping, the presents were quickly loaded. As Martha Lou drove away, Ruth called Penny back into the house. The Yorkie pranced past her, head held high, and made straight for her yellow bed. Too much going on in the household for one morning. Time for a well-earned nap.

Ruth and Sarah headed back to the kitchen to prepare lunch for sixteen people. At least that's the number Ruth had come up with after counting imaginary noses. She'd kept the menu simple. Lasagna, salad, and garlic bread. Brownies for dessert. The lasagna was already put together and in the refrigerator, ready for baking. She just needed to do the salad and brownies. And set the table. And make iced tea.

And try not to worry about Ben and Christina, who *still* hadn't come out of the guestroom.

The phone rang. It was Maddy, saying they'd picked up Keith and Dora, and were on their way back.

"They're in high spirits, as usual." Maddy laughed. Ruth could hear her brother and Don chortle in the background. "Teasin' all the way. Aunt Dora's got this pink striped dress on with matchin' shoes. Uncle Keith says — "

"I came with my walkin' bottle a Pepto Bismol!" Keith yelled loudly enough for Ruth to hear. "In case I eat too much weddin' cake."

More laughter in Ruth's ear, including Dora's *hahahahaha*. Dora was always a great sport. Ruth giggled in spite of herself. "That's not very nice."

Maddy's voice faded. "She's says that's not very nice, Uncle Keith."

"You know the truth hurts!" Keith again. And more guffawing.

"Okay, Mama." Maddy sounded almost giddy. "See ya soon."

Ruth hung up the phone, shaking her head.

"I could hear them from over here." Sarah stood at a drawer across the kitchen, gathering utensils.

"They're in quite a mood." Ruth pulled out the mixer to make the brownies. Had Maddy and Don warned them about Edna yet? Surely they had. But knowing her brother and sister-in-law, they'd just try to laugh their way through any disaster.

Maybe that's what the family needed.

A minute later she was getting eggs out of the refrigerator when Christina and Ben appeared. Ruth stilled. Sarah stopped her work at the sink.

Ruth searched Christina's face. Her eyes were red. *Oh no.* "You okay?" Both of the kids looked so grim.

Ben took Christina's hand. "We need to go to the airport to get Tanya and Jamie."

Ruth nodded. Wasn't it a little early for them to leave? "You can take my car."

Christina started to say something, then hesitated. She pulled her top lip between her teeth. "We're stopping at the motel on the way. I'm going to tell my mother she needs to leave."

A mixture of relief and sadness swirled through Ruth.

"She broke her promise. I just can't have her here if she's going to ... act like that." Christina took a breath. "I'm sorry all this happened. I'm really, really sorry." Her voice wavered.

Ruth set down the eggs. "You don't have to be sorry. This is *your* weekend. We all just want it to go well for you."

She nodded.

"You sure that's what you want to do?"

Christina raised her chin. "I made the decision, not Ben. I was afraid to at first. But I'm *tired* of being pushed around."

Ruth hid her surprise. Christina typically didn't share her emotions.

"Thing is, I'm not sure she'll go." Christina swallowed. What if she didn't? "I'll pray for you."

"Thanks, Mom." Ben gave her a tired smile.

"Yes, thanks." Christina's voice was tight. "We'll need it."

CHAPTER 17

Carrying her small purse, Jess limped over the threshold into Henry Curd's house, still mad enough to spit. Behind her at the curb sat Tamel's ridiculous banana yellow hearse—his everyday car. Only Tamel Curd would take a black hearse, paint it yellow, and *drive* the thing. Jess was ready to make a snide comment about it—for the hundredth time—until she got a glance at Tamel. He looked like he hadn't slept in a week. Hair not combed, circles under his eyes.

"Hey." She hugged him, and he didn't want to let go. When she stepped back he tried to smile. His incredible dimples appeared, but his lips were crooked.

He gestured toward her leg. "You limpin'?"

"Not really. Just looks like it."

"What happened?"

"My foot got in the way of Edna's motel door."

Tamel raised his eyebrows. "You went to see her?"

"Yeah. To run her outta town." Jess sighed.

Tamel nodded slowly. "I take it that didn't work."

"You could say that." Jess looked around the dingy living room. "Where's your dad?"

"Sleepin'. He had a bad night."

"Which means *you* had a bad night."

Tamel shrugged. "It happens."

Jess's limbs suddenly felt weighted. Tamel's tiredness was catching. But wasn't that the way it had been since they got together last July? She *felt* his emotions. He felt hers. They were bound by an unseen cord, whether she was here in Justus or home in Memphis.

The thought warmed Jess. It also scared her to death.

"Come on." Tamel nudged her toward the couch. "Let's sit down. You want some coffee?"

"No." Her to-go cup from Mocha Ritaville sat untouched in her car. "But looks like you could use some."

"Yeah."

They headed into the kitchen. Jess sat at the table while Tamel rinsed out the coffee carafe. She set her purse on the floor.

"I got Lois Stanton lined up to watch Dad today so I can come to the rehearsal and supper." Tamel measured grounds into a white filter.

"What about tomorrow for the weddin'?"

"He wants to come."

Jess pulled her head back. "Can he?"

"No. But he won't admit it. You watch, tomorrow he'll expect me to help him get dressed."

"What are you goin' to do?"

Tamel pushed the coffee maker to *on* and turned to face Jess. "Lois is lined up again. I just haven't told him."

"What if he argues?"

"Too bad. Besides, for once he doesn't have the strength to fight me."

Jess's heart panged. Tamel sounded so ... defeated.

He folded his arms and leaned against the counter. "Do you think it was the right thing to do, goin' to Edna Day?"

"I had to try. The woman's a walkin' nightmare."

"But was it your place? Why not Christina?"

"She doesn't have the guts."

"It's *her* mother."

"It's *my* brother."

Tamel lifted a shoulder. "Jess, you can't always take on the world."

"She's not the world. She's one woman. And a poor excuse for one at that." Jess folded her arms. Why was Tamel arguing with her? Like she hadn't been through enough this morning. "And how dare she show up in the first place! She knew she wasn't invited."

"Maybe she just wants to see her daughter get married. That's a pretty important day."

"Yeah, well, she had a lot of important days with her daughter. Like a whole *childhood*. She didn't seem to care about any of *them*."

"I know." Tamel busied himself with checking the coffee maker. Liquid was still running into the carafe.

"And besides, this isn't just about Christina. It's about Ben — and my whole family."

"I get that."

"Then *why* are you sayin' I shouldn't have gone?"

Tamel sighed. "I wasn't tellin' you. I was merely askin'."

"Sounded pretty accusatory to me."

Tamel raised both hands. "Okay. Fine. I'm not sayin' another word."

Jess glared at the table. What was *wrong* with the man this morning? Tamel usually had a way of rolling through anything. "You have any idea what I just went through, confrontin' Lady Godzilla? Not to mention my parents' household, which is in a total uproar—all because this woman thinks she can just waltz in and take over. Way things are goin', this weddin's gonna be a total disaster. And you just want me to sit back and do nothin' about it."

Tamel took a long breath. He rubbed his forehead. "Maybe I can help."

"Oh, really. How?"

"Maybe I can talk to her. Calm her down."

Now that was funny. "Do tell."

He shrugged. "Nobody else seems to be able to handle her."

"The woman doesn't 'handle' like some trained dog, Tamel. Besides, I don't want you anywhere near her."

"Why?"

"'Cause you're male and you're hot, that's why. She'll be all over you like a fly on cake. And then I really would have to kill her."

Tamel gazed at Jess—then suddenly grinned. There went his dimples again. Dratted man. Just when she was getting worked up.

He sidled over to the table and pulled her to her feet. Pain shot through her toes. "Really? I'm hot?"

She wrapped a hand around the back of his neck. "Hasn't Rita Betts told you so a million times?"

Tamel ran a finger against her cheek. "Just so you know—Rita doesn't have one thing over you."

"Wow, now *that's* a compliment."

"You're welcome." He brought his face closer and kissed her, long and slow.

Jess leaned into Tamel, letting herself drown in the feel of him. He tasted sweet and good. Like forever should taste. How she could get lost in this man. She, who wasn't supposed to get lost in anybody.

They pulled apart. Jess laid her head on Tamel's shoulder.

"Not mad at me anymore?" He stroked her hair.

"*You* were the one mad at *me*."

"Huh-uh. Never."

"Fine then."

The coffee gurgled to a stop.

Jess sat back down in her chair while Tamel poured himself a cup. He took a seat opposite her. "Did I tell you my dad's latest idea about the funeral home?"

Selfish Henry Curd couldn't let go of the notion that Tamel should remain in Justus forever and run his ratty business. "Now what?"

One side of Tamel's mouth curved. "He wants me to install a drive-through for viewings."

Jess lowered her chin. "He wants you to *what*?"

"You know, like a bank drive-through. You never have to get out of your car to pay your respects."

"That's the dumbest idea I ever heard! Who'd ever *do* that?"

Tamel laughed. "He said he's heard about other homes doin' it."

"Like where, exactly?"

"I don't remember, some small town up North."

"Hmph." Jess couldn't imagine such a thing ever flying in the South. "I don't care *who* does it, it's still a terrible idea. You call drivin' by some window 'payin' respects?' You're supposed to comfort the *family*. You're there for them, not the deceased."

Jess could feel herself getting worked up all over again. Then she caught the smile on Tamel's face. "Oh, you! You're totally makin' this up."

"Am not."

"Are too."

"No really, I'm not. I thought Dad was goin' bonkers, so I googled it. Sure enough I found a picture of an open casket—empty—on the other side of a huge drive-up window."

Oh, good grief. "So what's the point of this so-called wonderful idea?"

"Dad's convinced it'll bring flocks of new customers as far away as Jackson."

"I see. Enough customers to keep you happy runnin' a funeral home in Justus for the rest of your life."

"That's the ticket."

"Well, that's just great."

"I'm seriously considerin' it."

"Uh-huh."

They eyed each other—then burst out laughing. Took them awhile to settle down.

"Oh, man." Jess leaned back in her chair. "We needed that."

Tamel nodded.

They fell quiet. Jess's thoughts returned to her fight with Edna. *I'll only leave if Christina tells me to.*

"Oh. I have to call Ben." Reaching for her phone in her purse, Jess told Tamel what Edna had said. "Not that I one hundred percent believe she'll stick to it, but it's worth a try." Jess tapped Ben's name on the cell. When he answered he sounded as worn as Tamel.

"Hi, Jess."

"Where are you?"

"In Mom's car on the way to the motel."

Oh. "To see Edna?"

"Yeah. Christina decided she wants her to go."

Well, what do you know. "Glad to hear it. I need to tell you—I've already been to see her."

"*What?* Why?"

"Like you have to ask."

"Jess you—." He blew out air. "You had no right to do that!"

"I just wanted to help you and Christina." Not to mention the whole family. And the town.

"You can *help* by stayin' out of this. Whether she stays or goes is Christina's call."

Jess pressed her lips together. Was she destined to argue with *everyone* today? "Fine, Ben. You go over there and handle it all by yourselves. I won't tell you what I was about to tell you—which might be helpful for you to know."

Silence. Tamel gave her a look—*Take it easy.* She ignored him.

"Okay, Jess." Ben's voice came over the line. "You win. What is it?"

"Just that Christina doesn't need to beat around the bush. Edna said she'd leave if her daughter told her to. So all Christina needs to do is tell her flat out and be done with it. No 'talking this out' stuff."

Which Christina could easily fall into again, just like she'd done last night.

"Okay. Good to know."

Ben didn't sound convinced. Truth was, Jess wasn't convinced either. Would Edna Day keep her word or become crazier than ever?

"We're almost at the motel," Ben said. "Gotta go."

"Good luck. She's in room 207, by the way."

Jess clicked off the call and looked at Tamel. "Wanna place bets on whether she leaves or not?"

CHAPTER 18

Ruth was setting the kitchen table when she heard the garage door go up. "They're here." She put down the stack of plates.

"Yup." Sarah turned off the oven. "Just in time, the lasagna's done."

"There goes our quiet." Syton grinned as he rose from his chair in the family room. He and Jake had just returned from Jackson, toting plastic bags of tuxedos. Jake had taken them into his and Sarah's room to stack on the bed.

Ruth glanced at Lady Penelope, who was still sleeping. Not for long.

"Jake, they're here!" Sarah called toward their bedroom.

"Comin'!"

Penny's head rose. She eyed Sarah as if to say *How dare you wake me?*

Sy entered the kitchen. "I'm not sure which one's louder, your brother or his wife."

"Oh, Sy." Ruth swatted his shoulder. "You know you love 'em."

He stole a quick kiss. "I love anything that comes with this territory."

Ruth smiled.

"Uncle Keith and Aunt Dora are here!" Pogey's voice came from the kids' play room. Ruth entered the west hall to see him trotting down toward the garage.

"Oh, candy, candy!" Lacey spilled out of the room next, followed by Alex.

Ruth called after her grandkids. "Now don't you go askin' for candy the minute you see them."

As if they had to ask. Keith and Dora were known to throw sweets into the air as they made their entrance. They'd owned a candy shop in Nashville for years and couldn't resist showering the kids in the family with their favorite pieces. They'd been unable to have children of their own.

The door to the garage opened and Dora bustled through. Her dress was sure enough hot pink with white stripes. Her shoes were just as bright, as was her purse. Dora's round face beamed as she spread her pudgy arms. "Ruthie! Sy! We heard there's a weddin' goin' on here. Can we come?"

Lacey, Alex, and Pogey jumped up and down and gave their Great Aunt Dora effusive hugs.

"You have candy?" Alex bounced on her toes.

"Candy? Me?"

"You know you do." Pogey peered around her at his Great Uncle Keith. "One of you does."

"Well, now we just might have somethin' for you."

"Pogey, mind your manners." Sarah's voice came from behind Ruth.

"Aw, it's fine." Dora waved her hand in the air.

"Where's that crazy family of mine?" Keith boomed the words as he stepped into the hall, Maddy and Don behind him. Keith looked over the heads of the kids, purposely ignoring them. "Ruthie? Sy?"

"What about *us*?" Alex ran around Dora and stopped in front of him. Lacey followed.

"Oh! And who are you? And you?"

The girls laughed and jumped some more.

"You know who we are."

"Come on, Uncle Keith."

Keith put his hands on his hips. "Who you callin' Uncle? I'm your *great* uncle, for your information. Emphasis on the *great*."

Everyone laughed. Ruth beckoned them forward. "Come on into the kitchen where I have room to hug you. Too many people in this hallway."

They all moved, the kids chattering, and Dora and Keith talking at once. Keith started pulling candy from his pockets and throwing them toward the family room. The girls squealed and scampered after the treasure, Pogey on their heels.

A long-suffering Penny watched from the safety of her bed.

Dora and Keith went around the circle, hugging Ruth and Sy, Sarah and Jake. Dora chattered about various people they'd seen in the airport and some "crazy gal" who sat beside her on the plane, while Keith countered all her explanations with descriptions of his own.

"Oh, go on, Keith." Dora wagged her head. "You know she had black hair, not brown."

"Curly too."

"Was not. Straight as a stick."

"And skinny."

"She was round as a butter ball, like me."

Keith lifted both hands in the air. "Whatever, woman."

113

Dora pulled in her mouth. "Don't you 'whatever woman' me." She turned to Ruth. "And buck teeth? Whooey, that gal could eat corn through a picket fence."

Don and Jake guffawed.

"Oooh, Hershey's Kiss, I want that one!" Alex grabbed for a chocolate in Lacey's hand. Lacey jerked it away.

"Alexandra, stop it right now." Maddy headed over to break up the argument.

"I had it first!"

"Oh, fine, go ahead." Lacey held out the chocolate to her cousin. "I'll take another one."

Maddy reached the girls. "Lacey, that's very nice of you, but Alex can get somethin' else."

"No I can't, I want *that* one!"

"Hey, hey!" Sy pointed at Alex. "You know the rules. No whinin'."

"But I—"

"*No* whinin'. Or I'll take all your candy and give it to Lacey and Pogey. That what you want?"

"Hear your granddad, Alex?" Don spoke from the kitchen.

Alex folded her arms and aimed one of her infamous pouts at her father.

Maddy tapped her daughter's puffed out lip. "Now that's a beautiful sight. You look mad as a wet hatter."

Ruth suppressed a giggle. Dora and Keith exchanged a confused glance.

Sarah laughed. "Hen, Maddy."

"Huh?"

"Mad as a wet hen."

Keith shrugged. "Unless she means mad as a hatter."

"Who's mad as a hatter?" Sy looked around.

"Not me," said Dora.

"Or me," said Don.

"I am *not* a hatter." Alex was still pouting.

"Maybe she meant stark ravin' mad," Keith teased.

Alex huffed. "I am *not* a raven!"

All the adults burst into laughter. Which only made Alex all the angrier.

Maddy raised both hands. "Will y'all stop makin' fun of me!"

"Me too!" Alex started to cry.

"Aw, now, Alex." Keith strode into the family room and swooped her up. He held her high by the waist, tipping her face down toward his. "Don't you know if you frown like that the candy tastes sour?" He puckered up his mouth.

Alex giggled. "No it doesn't."

"Oh, yes it does." He frowned all the harder, sending Alex into chortles of laughter. After twirling her around, he set her down and buffed her head.

"Oww!"

"Oh, get out, that didn't hurt."

Keith turned from Alex and spotted Lady Penelope. "Well, hey there, Miss Princess."

Uh-oh, Ruth thought. Keith had always been far too loud for Penny.

The Yorkie turned a cold shoulder.

"Ignorin' me again, are ya?"

"Keith, you know how it goes." Ruth picked up plates to finish setting the table. "Let her be, and she'll come to you when she's good and ready."

"Uh-huh. Eternity's comin', too."

Ruth set down a plate. It was sure going to be a crowded table, even without the kids. They'd been eating in the family room. "Oh. Sarah, would you call Jess? Tell her it's time for lunch."

"Sure." Sarah headed for the kitchen phone.

Dora plopped down in a chair at the table and set her purse on the floor. "So where is Jess?"

"With Tamel," Ruth said. "Her boyfriend."

"Oh, yes." Dora drew out the words. "She gonna marry that boy?"

Ruth picked up a handful of silverware. "Better not go talkin' marriage to Jessica. She'll just laugh at you."

"Well." Dora tilted her head. "There are laughs, and there are *laughs*, know what I mean? Maybe that independent girl of yours just doesn't wanna face the fact that she needs somebody."

Wasn't that the truth. "Maybe."

Sarah hung up the phone. "She's comin'."

"And where's the happy couple?" Dora asked.

Ruth set silverware at her place. "Off to Jackson to pick up Tanya and Jamie—the best man and maid of honor."

Well, at least they *would* be on their way to Jackson—after seeing Edna Day. Ruth sent up what must have been her dozenth prayer that God would help Christina through the confrontation.

"Will they be here for lunch?"

"Second shift." Ruth smiled.

Dora glanced at the kids and lowered her voice. "How're they doin'? Maddy told us about Christina's mother showin' up."

"They're all right. Sounds like she won't be at the weddin' after all. Christina's askin' her to leave."

Dora raised her penciled eyebrows. "Think it's that simple?"

Ruth shook her head. "Hope so. For everyone's sake. Especially Christina's."

"From what Maddy said ... I mean, what if she doesn't go?"

Ruth straightened and let out a sigh. "Then we're in for a very interestin' time."

Dora let out a sudden yawn. "Oh, mercy. Sorry. Trip musta wore me out." She reached into her purse and pulled out a small plastic bag of brown ... things.

Ruth frowned at it. "What's that?"

"Shhh." Dora threw a glance at her husband. "Chocolate covered espresso beans, infused with a whole lot of extra caffeine. Keith doesn't like me eatin' 'em. Says they make me crazier than I already am. *I* say they keep me awake."

Pogey looked up from his place on the family room floor. Pieces of candy were scattered around him. He reached for a roll of Sweet Tarts.

"I heard that, woman." Keith pushed back from Penny's bed and stood. "You watch, Ruthie. Now she'll be as wound up tighter 'n' a two-dollar watch."

"I want one!" Pogey held up the Sweet Tarts. "Trade ya this for it, Aunt Dora."

"No way, Pogey," Sarah called from the kitchen. "Those things are off the charts in caffeine."

"Don't forget the sugar." Dora looked pleased with herself. "Quite the combination, you ask me." She dropped the bag into her purse. "But don't you worry. This is my own private little stash."

As Ruth began to cut pieces of lasagna, the conversation rattled on. Dora just had to tell everyone about their new neighbor, who was either "ex CIA" or "watched too many movies." And of course Keith had to add his two cents, disagreeing with all his wife's descriptions until she threatened to bop him over the head. The kids were getting along again, now bartering over their pieces of candy. And Penny had eased from her bed to join them. Ruth loved the flow of family around her. She smiled as she plated up the lasagna and salad. By the wedding tomorrow, Sy's two sisters and their families would be in town. It would be a gathering like they hadn't seen in a long time.

But in the back of her mind sat Worry, like some ugly creature ready to pounce. Worry for Christina. And Ben. Edna too. The woman had to be carrying hurts of her own. But she was also a loose cannon. And if she showed up at the wedding, who knew what she might do.

CHAPTER 19

By the time Ben pulled into a parking place at the motel, Christina's heart was pounding. She took a couple of deep breaths. Why should she be so scared at the mere thought of talking to her mother? She'd managed to get through last night, hadn't she? Had even said a few things she'd thought she would never say.

Ben shut off the engine and clicked open his door. "You ready?"

Christina hesitated. "You're going with me?"

"Of course."

She wasn't sure how to feel about that.

"Christina, I'm not lettin' you go up there alone."

She gazed out the windshield. "It's not your job to do this."

"I didn't say it was my job. I said I'm goin' with you. My *job* is to stay by your side when you need me."

Christina lowered her eyes. She was tired of her swirling emotions. In the space of one second she could

119

feel two totally opposite things. At the moment she wanted Ben with her—and she didn't.

His voice firmed. "Christina."

She ran one thumb over another. "I think I need to do this alone."

"Huh-uh. Not happenin'."

"I … She needs to see this is coming just from me. That you're not putting me up to it."

"She could think that just as easily with me waitin' for you in the car."

"I know, but …"

"Christina, I'm comin'. Now let's go do this."

She took another deep breath. Let it out.

"Listen to me." Ben cupped her chin. "I know this is about you and your history, and your childhood. But it's also about our life together. Our future. And don't forget—it's my weddin', too."

"I *know* that."

"Then what are you waitin' for?"

Christina's eyes grew moist. How to explain to him when she didn't understand it all herself? And what if they went through their entire marriage like this? As much as Ben loved her, he would never fully realize what she'd been through, not with his perfect, loving childhood. He *couldn't.*

She blinked back the tears. "I'm scared."

Ben's expression softened—a look of love that pierced her heart. "That's why I'm goin' with you."

With Ben beside her, Christina could do anything. Her fear receded a little, like a slow-moving tide. In place of the ebbing waters lay only sand. But it was wet sand, hard and packed. Ground she could walk on without stumbling.

"Okay."

They climbed the motel stairs to the second floor in silence.

Ben stood back as Christina knocked on the door. Her hand shook.

No answer.

"Mom! It's me."

An eternity passed before she heard footsteps. The door opened. Her mother stood before her in an old blue T-shirt and a pair of gray pajama bottoms. Her hair was messy, and mascara smeared her eyes.

Christina knew the look. The morning after a night of drinking.

They stared at each other. Edna Day's focus moved over Christina's shoulder to Ben.

"Well, what a nice surprise." Her voice croaked. "Wanna come in?"

"That's okay." Christina laced her trembling hands. "This'll just take a minute."

Her mother raised her chin slowly, as if preparing herself. "I see. What can I do you for?"

Christina licked her lips. She felt Ben's touch on her back. "You need to go. Last night I made it clear you couldn't drink if you wanted to stay. That was our bargain. You broke it. So now you need to leave."

There. She'd done it. Staked out her boundary. Christina's pulse beat even harder.

Pain creased her mother's face. "You're tellin' your own mother she ain't allowed at your weddin'? After I came all the way here and spent hard earned money on a motel room?"

Ben's touch felt warm. Assuring.

"Which, by the way, is reserved for tonight and tomorrow night. And I prob'ly can't get out of it now without payin' for it."

121

Christina's gaze dropped. She took a moment to steel herself, then raised her eyes again. "You didn't keep your promise."

Her mother wrapped a hand around the doorframe. One of her sparkling purple fingernails was broken. "I just had a few drinks, that's all. Nothin' to keep me from showin' up tomorrow. Sober."

Christina felt her head shake. "No. We had a deal."

"But if I don't come, who's gonna walk you down the aisle?"

Christina blinked. "Down the aisle?"

"Your father's gone, rest his soul. You got no brothers or uncles around, leastways no uncles that care. What're you plannin' on doin', walkin' down the aisle all by yourself?"

That was exactly what Christina had planned—because she had no choice. No way would she want her mother by her side. Ever.

"Yes, by myself. And I'm fine with that."

"You don't want me to give you away?"

A dark laugh rose in Christina's throat. "Give me *away?*" She shook her head. "You did that long ago."

Her mother's eyes narrowed. "How come you're so judgmental all of a sudden? I thought Christians were supposed to forgive. And *you.*" Edna looked to Ben. "Standin' behind my daughter, like you don't have the nerve to face me yourself. Some man you got there, Chris."

Rage shot through Christina, chasing away what remained of her fright. Ben gripped her shoulder, his own anger radiating from his skin. "Her *name,*" he spat, "is *Christina.*"

"I can call her whatever I want. *I* gave birth to her."

"That's about *all* you did for her."

"What you can call me"—Christina pointed at her mother—"is *gone.*"

The rage bounced around her rib cage. And it felt good. *Good.* It gave her strength.

"I don't have to stand here and talk to you. I don't have to welcome you here, just because you came. I don't have to allow you to come to the wedding. I *didn't* invite you—for a very good reason. Because I knew you'd act like this. I knew you'd get drunk and embarrass me and everyone around you." Christina's voice was rising, but she couldn't stop it. Not now. Not after the years of abuse. "And you're *not* going to change my mind, no matter what you say. You can be mad. You can beg. You can even cry. It. Won't. Matter. Because you're not going to destroy my life any longer. And you're not going to wreck my wedding, the one day I've dreamed of for years—even as my father told me I'd never see it because no one would ever want me. And *you* laughed." Tears scratched at Christina's eyes, but she would not cry. "Well guess what. The day *has* come. And *you* won't see it."

The words ran out. Just like that Christina's anger faded, and she couldn't get it back. The sand beneath her started to loosen. Ben still gripped her shoulder. She could feel the love and pride in his fingers. Christina took a step back from her mother and leaned into him.

Edna Day's eyes were wide and shining, her mouth a long O. She stared at Christina as if she'd never seen her before.

Then her expression veiled. A sneer twisted her lips, even as a tear fell on her cheek. "Must feel good to speak your piece, *Christina.* Even if it is at the expense of your mother. Hope you're proud of yourself."

Another tear fell. *Why* was she crying? Part of Christina wanted to catch the tear in a bottle. Hold it up

123

to the light to prove her mother did love her. The other part wanted to smack it away. If anyone deserved to cry, it was *her*.

Christina swallowed. "I expect you to go home today."

Her mother tilted her head. "You can't tell me what to do. Neither can that sister of yours." She gestured toward Ben. "It's a free country."

"I don't want you here."

"I wanted to give you my weddin' present."

"You can give it to me now."

"Well, I ... It's not ready yet. I need to put it together."

Right. Like she really had a present.

"Look." Edna Day stuck a hand in her hair. "We can fix this. There's still a chance."

The words rocked Christina. *A chance to fix it.*

How amazing that her mother was admitting there was something to fix. All her life Christina had wanted a new beginning, with parents who would love her and care for her. Who would ask about her day at school. A mother who'd bake cookies. A father who wouldn't shame her in front of her friends. A house where she could have girls over for the night, and birthday parties and Christmases with joy instead of pain.

Could this wedding, this huge change in her life, possibly be the thing that could bring her mother around? Give them a chance to mend the past? Christina's counselor had told her that at some point she would need to completely forgive.

She squeezed her eyes shut. Still, forgiving didn't mean forgetting. It was an act of will, a letting go. But sometimes it had to come with boundaries for the sake of safety and peace.

Besides, she *had* given her mom another chance. Last night.

Christina straightened her back. *Dear God, please help me say the right words.*

"I hope we do have another chance, Mom. I want that, I pray for that. But not now. Not tomorrow, at my wedding. Sometime ... later. When you stop drinking. When you start thinking about anyone other than yourself."

Edna Day's face hardened. She smeared away the tears with the back of her hand. "What a selfish daughter you've turned out to be. I'm askin' you for a second chance, and you shoo me away like a stray dog. *Fine* then. I don't want to be at your stupid weddin' anyway, with all those people turnin' up their noses at me." She took a step backward. "Hope you're happy with your choice, *Christina*, because you'll never see me again. Have a great day and an oh-so-perfect life."

She slammed the motel door.

CHAPTER 20

Christina cried all the way to the airport.

Ben drove with one hand, the other on her arm. Typically he could just roll with things, but right now he wanted to hit something. More like some*one*. As if it wasn't enough for Edna Day to destroy her daughter's childhood. Now she had to destroy her wedding weekend, too?

"I'm sorry," Christina said for the tenth time.

"You don't have to be sorry. *I'm* sorry for *you*."

They reached their exit.

With an effort Christina straightened. She looked so tired. "I'm done crying now. Really. Because I've just … had it. And we're almost there."

"Okay."

"I don't want Tanya and Jamie to see me cry. What a way to be on the day before your wedding."

Christina's eyes were so red, they'd surely know she was upset. "They'd understand," Ben said.

She lifted her chin. "I'm done."

Relief trickled through Ben, and he felt himself relax a little. "I'm glad." Maybe now they could just get on with the weekend.

Christina's cell rang. She pulled it from her purse. "It's Tanya." Her finger hit the speakerphone button. "Hey, where are you?"

"Here! We got our bags and are heading out the door."

Christina looked to Ben.

"Two minutes, Tanya!" He aimed the words toward the phone. "Just come on outside, and we'll find you."

"Okay. I should tell you—Jamie's kinda sick."

Christina drew in a breath. "Oh, no, what's wrong?"

"It started on the flight. Like maybe the flu or something?"

Oh, wonderful. Get rid of the mother-in-law, and in walks the flu.

Christina's shoulders fell. "I'm so sorry. We'll take care of him. See you in a minute."

She clicked off the line and stared at her lap. "I can't believe this."

Frustration roiled through Ben. They'd planned their day to be so perfect. *Why* couldn't something go right? He wanted to pound the dashboard. Instead he patted Christina's arm. "It'll be okay."

She sighed, then nodded. "Yeah. Sure."

"Hey." Ben forced his tone to lighten. "We'll laugh about all this someday. Years from now, when we're tellin' our kids about our weddin'."

Christina leaned back against the headrest. "Think so?"

"I know so."

They reached the area to pick up passengers. Ben drove slowly, looking for Tanya and Jamie among the milling arrivals. He recognized Tanya's blonde curls first.

128

Jamie was sitting on his suitcase, slumped over. He looked like he'd been hit by a truck.

Great. Just great.

"There they are." Ben pulled to the curb.

Christina unfastened her seatbelt. "Know what we'll tell our kids? We should have eloped."

CHAPTER 21

Jess heard the noise level in her parents' house before she even entered the front door. Her toes still hurt, but she did her best to walk normally. She entered the family room to find the three kids on the floor, eating lasagna and arguing some inane detail about the wedding. The rest of the family was stuffed around the elongated kitchen table. Sarah was chuckling—apparently over something Maddy had said. Aunt Dora and Uncle Keith volleyed jabs at each other. Jess's dad was talking to Don, and her mom was smiling but looked like she just wanted to put her hands over her ears.

"Hi, everyone."

"Hey, Jess!" her aunt and uncle sang. They rose to give her hugs, yakking about how good she looked, and where was that man of hers, and how was the law firm, and on and on. And goodness, was she *limping?*

The whole family considered her feet.

"No, no, I'm just fine." By the time Jess got a piece of lasagna and some salad, and squeezed into a place at the corner of the table, her ears rang. And her stupid foot still hurt.

Good grief, had the family always been this loud?

Aunt Dora launched into a story about some old couple who snored through church, Uncle Keith adding embellishments. Not a word was being said about Edna Day, as if that sword of Damocles didn't hang over all their heads.

And what had happened when Ben and Christina went to see the woman? Jess hadn't heard a word.

Across the table, Jess's mom raised questioning eyebrows. Jess shrugged—*I don't know.*

The kitchen phone rang. Jess rose to answer since she was closest, making sure she didn't limp. She could barely hear Ben's voice on the other end. Whatever it was, he didn't sound happy.

"Hey, y'all!" She shooshed the family with a wave of her hand. "Quiet!"

Alex's voice rose from the family room. "Well, *I* say you throw the flowers in big bunches."

"No you don't," Lacey said. "You spread them out little by little."

"Hey, kids!" Jess held the phone away from her face. "Knock it off for a minute, would ya?"

They fell quiet.

Oh, the sound of silence.

Jess replaced the phone to her ear. "Now what, Ben?"

"We got Tanya and Jamie. Jamie's sick. He thinks it's somethin' he ate. We had to stop twice already so he could get out and throw up."

"Oh, no."

"If it is food poisoning, he should be better by tomorrow. But he's too sick to leave by himself at the motel room. And he sure doesn't want to so much as smell food. Tell Mom I'm gonna bring him through the front door and straight upstairs to my bed. He can stay there tonight. I'll sleep on the couch."

Poor Jamie. Why did *he* have to get food poisoning? Why not Edna? "This is terrible. The rehearsal's at four o'clock." Less than three hours from now.

"Jamie won't be there, that's for sure."

Poor Ben. And Christina. What was *happening* with this wedding? "Okay. I'll tell Mom."

Jess glanced at her family around the table. The ones facing her were watching with *now-what?* expressions. The rest clearly had their ears pricked. So did the kids.

She walked into the dining room and lowered her voice. "How did it go with Edna?"

"Not good."

"What does that mean?"

"We'll talk about it later." Stress coated Ben's reply. So unlike him.

Without another word, he hung up.

Jess took the receiver from her ear and stared at it.

CHAPTER 22

Walking into the kitchen with Tanya, Christina forced a smile on her face. Ben was hauling a weak Jamie up to his bedroom. Christina told herself she'd get through this. She just needed a positive attitude. And some time by herself to regroup. Which she wasn't about to get.

The family greeted Christina with warm hugs and I'm-sorrys about Jamie, including the aunt and uncle she hadn't met — Dora and Keith. Christina introduced Tanya to everyone. "My best friend at work. The one in the cubicle next to mine, who keeps me sane."

Hellos and welcomes all around, and a big hug for Tanya from Mama Ruth. Tanya threw Christina one of her looks — *they're wonderful, just like you said.*

"Tanya, come sit down here, and I'll get you some lasagna." Ruth gestured to her own chair. "I'm done anyway."

Sarah got up as well, offering her chair to Christina.

"You're every bit as beautiful as I've heard, Christina." Aunt Dora beamed at her.

She felt her face flush. "Thank you."

"Tanya," Mama Ruth said, "I hear you have pictures and stuffed animals of giraffes all over your cubicle at work."

"Yes, ma'am."

Aunt Dora rubbed her hands together. "Let me tell you about the time Keith and I went to the zoo before we got married ..."

And the woman was off and running on some story of how the wind blew a straw hat off her head, which a giraffe promptly picked up and started eating. Soon the whole family was laughing, one story leading to another. Christina ate her lasagna and let the conversation flow around her, smiling, smiling. More than once she raised her eyebrows at Tanya, whose head swiveled back and forth at each comment. Typical behavior for the Dearings. But Christina felt it in the air—a sense that they knew how terrible the day was going for her, and they'd determined before she ever walked in the door to raise her spirits.

Where was her mother right now? In her car, headed back to Austin? Or still at the motel, defiant and full of revenge.

Sadness knifed through Christina. Any dream she'd had of fixing things with her mother had melted as she and Ben had driven away from that motel. Edna Day would never forgive her for this.

Uncle Keith made some comment that Christina missed, and everybody laughed. She smiled all the more.

Ben joined the noisy group, sitting next to Christina in the chair Maddy gave up for him. He squeezed Christina's knee. "Jamie's in bed."

"Poor guy." Ruth placed a plate of lasagna and salad in front of Ben.

"Yeah. Good thing I got my own bathroom, 'cause he surely needs it."

Jess winced at that.

After lunch Sarah pulled Christina into the living room. "How are you? Really?"

Christina's eyes suddenly burned. *No, no, no.* She wasn't going there. She raised her chin and tried to smile. "Fine."

Sarah gazed at Christina, clearly seeing through her. She sighed. "Yeah. Thought so." She drew Christina into a hug.

Not until they pulled apart did Christina notice all the wedding gifts were gone. "They're all packed up?"

"Yup, all taken care of. Next thing you know, they'll be arrivin' at your apartment about the time you get back from your honeymoon."

Gratitude swept through Christina. She may have had unloving parents, but look at the incredible family she was marrying into.

Her thoughts flashed to her Christian counselor a month ago, reading Bible verses from the book of Joel. Chapter two talked about Israel in a day of terror, defenseless, quaking, and devastated. Like Christina as a child, locked in a closet. Or lying on her bed, leg welts throbbing from her father's belt. But, said the verses, the Lord would change things completely. He would make up to Israel for "the years that the swarming locust has eaten." Then Israel's fields would sprout new growth, and the people would eat well and be satisfied. And they would praise God, who had dealt wondrously with them. And they would *never again be put to shame.*

That's what God was doing for her, right here, right now. With this family.

"Thank you, Sarah, so much. For taking care of our gifts and … everything."

Sarah waved a hand. "You deserve it."

No she didn't, not at all.

They headed back into the kitchen, where the other women were cleaning up. Tanya was on the floor in the family room, holding Penny and chatting away with the three kids, who already seemed enamored with her. Ben's dad sat in his armchair, chuckling over some story Uncle Keith was telling. Jake and Don were laughing as well. Ben was gone. Probably upstairs, checking on Jamie.

Ruth wouldn't let Christina help with the dishes. "No, you and Ben go on. Don't you want to get Tanya checked into the motel before the rehearsal?"

Christina hesitated. Yes, they did. But what if they ran into her mother?

Ruth saw her expression and nodded. "Maybe Ben should just take her."

"I'll take her when I'm done here." Jess turned from her work at the sink. "We'll just get her things in the room and come right back."

Christina eyed her. Part of Jess was trying to be helpful, no doubt. The other part surely wanted to check for signs of the woman she'd tried to run out of town that morning.

Jess raised her eyebrows, all innocence.

"Thanks," Christina said.

She joined Tanya on the floor, trying to filter out the men's voices as Tanya asked the kids about their lives and school, and if Pogey had a girlfriend. Which made him blush. Lacey's eyes went wide.

"*You* have a girlfriend?"

Pogey shot her a withering older brother look. "She just asked a question, Lacey, doesn't mean it's true."

138

"Aw!" Uncle Keith turned from his own conversation. "Pogey, you got a *girlfriend*?"

Oh, boy, here we go.

"I do *not*!"

Tanya looked to Christina and spread her hands— *what have I done?*

"Hear that over there, Dora?" Uncle Keith called. "Pogey's just ... how old are you Pogey, ten? And he's already got a girlfriend."

Pogey's face was red. "I had my birthday in September. I'm eleven. And I *do not have a girlfriend*."

Ben's dad creased his face in animated confusion. "Then what are we talkin' about one for?"

"We're *not* talkin', Tanya just asked me, is all."

Don shook his head. "She musta had a reason to ask."

"Yeah," said Jake. "Son, what're you holdin' back?"

"Oh, Jake." Sarah held a plate and dishtowel in her hands. "Leave him alone."

"Yeah, hear that?" Pogey folded his arms. "Everybody leave me alone!"

Penny wriggled in Tanya's arms until Tanya put her down. The Yorkie trotted over to Pogey and gazed at him with understanding eyes. He picked her up.

Tanya's gaze flicked from person to person, her mouth crooked in a bemused expression.

Christina shrugged. "I told you they were crazy."

Everyone looked surprised at the un-Christina-like words. Then they burst out laughing. Christina laughed too.

It felt good.

Dishes done, Jess headed to the motel with Tanya. Christina waited nervously for their return, trying not to show it. Ben was in and out of the kitchen twice, fetching a glass of ice water for Jamie, then asking Mama Ruth in low tones for some medicine to stop "the trots."

139

Mama Ruth cocked her head in sympathy. "Is he throwin' up, too?"

By now everyone was listening for the intimate details.

"Oh yeah. He's got it comin' out both ends."

Christina cringed. Ben's dad stretched one side of his mouth at Uncle Keith.

Ruth pulled a bottle out of a cupboard and handed it to Ben, giving him instructions on dosage. Ben disappeared upstairs again.

A minute later Jess and Tanya returned. Christina locked onto Jess's face, holding her breath. Jess saw her expression and gave a slight shake of her head.

Relief flooded Christina. When Jess walked by she whispered, "You didn't even see her car there?"

"No." Jess shook her head.

Christina let the words sink in. Maybe the car was still parked at the bar from last night. Come to think of it, she hadn't noticed it when she and Ben were at the motel. Or maybe her mom really had gone.

The thought blew her relief away like dandelion dust.

How strange.

In its place came ... nothing. Just emptiness.

Then Ben returned to her side and slipped an arm around her shoulder, giving her one of his loving gazes. Aunt Dora went off on another silly story that had everyone laughing, and the kids headed down the hall toward their play room. Lady Penelope nuzzled up to Christina with a contented sigh. Christina ran her fingers through the silky fur, feeling the doggy warmth, and Ben's closeness, and the family love swirling around her.

In her mind rose a picture of a field in new growth.

CHAPTER 23

In her old bedroom suite upstairs Jess brushed her teeth and reapplied pale pink lipstick. It was three-forty. In a few minutes her mom would round up the troops for the wedding rehearsal at the church. Jamie still languished in Ben's bedroom next door. Every once in a while Jess could hear the toilet flush.

Ugh.

Before she went downstairs she took a few minutes to lie down and gather her thoughts. Thank goodness her foot had stopped hurting. She'd be able to go on her usual run tomorrow morning. Jess laced her hands and stared across the room at the rope handle hanging from the pull-down door to the attic. How many nights as a small child had she lain here, gazing at that rope, her mind conjuring hidden monsters? Jess smiled at the memories of calling out to her mother, who would come in and soothe her.

"There are no monsters up there, honey. I promise. Want to see? I'll take you up there."

Up there in the *dark?* Jess would shiver and shake her head. But one sunny day when she was six years old her father insisted on taking her into the attic.

"Come on, Jess, I'll go up first." He pulled down the stairs without waiting for her reply and climbed up. Tilting back her head, Jess saw a light come on. There was a *light* up there?

"All right. Your turn." Her father smiled down at her.

Ankles trembling, Jess mounted the stairs.

The attic was huge, running the entire length of the house. Even her dad could stand up in it, although beams crossed every five feet or so, making him duck. Jess's dad led her down the length of the attic, pointing out various boxes. "Over there's all the Christmas stuff. And these are boxes full of old letters and pictures your mom just can't let go of. See that long white box down there?"

Jess nodded.

"That's your mama's weddin' dress, packed away and ready to wear again."

Jess's mouth rounded to an O. "Who's gonna wear it?"

Her dad shrugged. "Well, your mama has three daughters. She's hopin' at least one will."

Sarah and Maddy had opted for their own dresses. Jess knew that box was still up there, unopened.

A sense of love and warmth flooded Jess. How fortunate she was to have such a family. And how glad she was that her parents still lived in the same house, even after all the kids moved away and her father retired, selling his car dealership. Jess couldn't imagine saying goodbye to this house and their family reunions.

And now—tomorrow—the family would grow by one more.

Jess closed her eyes and thanked God for all she had. *And, Jesus, I know I don't talk to you often enough. I tend to get on my high horse and want to take care of things myself. But could you please take care of this wedding for Ben and Christina? Just ... let it go well. Give them a good start —*

"Jess!" Ben's voice filtered from outside her door. "Time to go."

"Comin'."

She rose and went downstairs.

CHAPTER 24

Ruth led the family into the church, where Judy Crenshaw was already waiting. Just getting across town had brought more than a little chaos, with who deciding to ride with whom, and Keith and Dora coming and then not coming, with finally Keith deciding he'd stay at the house and check on Jamie once in a while—Jamie was still throwing up—and Dora would go. Plus, Keith declared, he would make friends with Penny if that was the last thing he did.

"It just might be," Sarah said. "If she turns her back on you and faces the corner, you're in trouble."

Maddy forgot the "bouquet" of ribbons-on-a-paper-plate from the shower and had to run back in the house to fetch it. Pogey was unhappy about having to practice walking down the aisle and was only placated at hearing from Sy that he wouldn't have to wear his "monkey suit" until the real wedding. Lacey and Alex were still arguing over how to throw the flowers from their baskets. Ruth finally had to quiet them, saying "Miss Judy" would explain what to do. Then both of the girls wanted Tanya to ride in their car, so that had to be sorted out. As for the bride and groom, they both wore expressions of weary excitement. Now that Edna Day had gone, maybe they could finally enjoy their own wedding.

And now here they were, all piling into the church. Ruth let out a sigh of relief.

Until Jess said, "Wait, Tamel's not here." She immediately called him, her face full of worry. "Is your dad all right? Are you comin'?"

"No" and "yes," replied Tamel. His dad was not in good shape, even worse than that morning, but Lois Stanton was there, shooing Tamel out the door and he'd be at the church in three minutes.

Which he was. Looking more than a little preoccupied, but at least he was present. Jess greeted him with a hug.

"All righty then." Judy Crenshaw clasped her hands at her waist. She looked pretty today as always, dressed in jeans and a red sweater that brought color to her face. "Looks like we're all here except Paul." Paul was her husband and pastor of the church, who would be conducting the ceremony. "He'll be here in a minute."

"Jamie's not here either," Alex spoke up. "He's got it comin' out both ends." She mugged at Lacey, clearly having no idea what that meant.

Titters ran through the group.

"Okaaaay." Judy couldn't help but laugh.

Ben explained the situation to Judy. "We're hopin' he's better by tomorrow."

"I see. Well. Anybody here not in the weddin'?"

"I'm not," Sy said.

"But you're bein' led in at the last with Ruthie. And Jamie's supposed to escort her."

146

Dora raised her hand. "How 'bout me?"

"Ah. Okay. Would you stand in for Jamie, please?"

"The best *man*?"

"You're all I've got."

Dora shrugged. "Sure, why not? I look just like him."

Lacey giggled.

"Okay then." Judy looked around the group. "All guests except Ruth will be seating themselves. As I said, when everyone else is seated, Jamie will escort her in. Sy, you'll follow."

Ruth felt a pang in her chest. She glanced at Christina. Her face remained neutral, but Ruth knew her mind had to be on her mother. This was the only wedding Ruth had seen that didn't need to reserve the left pews for the bride. It was the reason so many people in town had been invited. Ben wanted the church full so Christina would feel the pain of her absent family as little as possible.

"Jamie will go back up the aisle," Judy continued. "Then he'll go out the front door and around the side to join the rest of you men. When the weddin' starts, y'all will enter through there." She pointed to a side door that led to the area behind the sanctuary. "So that's where you need to go now. All women and the kids—out to the vestibule. Ruthie and Sy, you'll be seated on the front row here, so you can go ahead and sit."

The family milled into two groups, eventually starting to make their way to their prospective places. But not without Don and Jake kidding Ben—again—about this being his last "free night on earth," and Ben saying "I know, I know." To which Christina shot him a look, which shut all three of them up. Meanwhile Sy started to head out the side door, and Ruth had to pull him back. "Hey, bud, you're with me."

147

"Oh, yeah, that's right." He raised both shoulders. "Just used to hangin' with the guys."

Judy pointed to Lacey and Alex, who were standing around looking lost. "Girls, you go on up the aisle too."

"Good grief." Maddy shook her head. "This is just like herdin' bats."

Sarah chortled. "*Cats*, Maddy."

Maddy looked around. "Cats? Where?"

All the adults burst out laughing, including Judy and Tanya. Lacey and Alex exchanged puzzled glances. Pogey didn't break a smile.

"I think she means we're all batty." Jake was half bent over, hands to his stomach.

"It's ..." Jess could hardly talk. "Herdin' *cats*."

Maddy planted her hands on her hips. Ruth knew her middle daughter all too well. Maddy knew she'd had another slip of the tongue, but she wasn't about to give in now. "Why would *anybody* want to herd cats?"

"Why would anybody want to herd *bats*?" Jess shot back.

"That's just the *point*. You *don't*."

"You don't herd cats, either."

Maddy rolled her eyes. "Oh, fine then. Whatever. Can we just do this thing?"

"Which one?" Sy spread his hands. "The cats or the bats?"

Another round of guffaws. That was too much for Maddy. She strode up the aisle and out the door.

"Oh, my goodness." Ruth had laughed so hard she felt tears in her eyes. "We'll never get this rehearsal done."

Dora couldn't stop giggling. "Talk about herdin' bats, I got an idea. Sy, why don't *you* be Jamie, and I'll be you."

Don turned to Jake, his cheeks red from laughing. "Yeah, and you and I can be each other."

148

"Right." Jake pointed around the group. "And Tamel can be Ruth, and Pogey, you be Ben."

Pogey drew back his head. "*I'm* not gettin' married."

"Why not, Pogey?" Don spread his hands. "You'd make a fine-lookin' groom."

"I got enough to do with carryin' the stupid rings."

That sour note brought all the laughter to a halt. Ruth frowned at him.

"Aw, now, Pogey." Jake buffed his son's head. "Straighten up. You want to do this for Ben and Christina, don't you? They're family."

Pogey glowered at his feet. "I guess."

"You guess?"

"Okay. Yeah." Pogey still sounded none too happy.

"That's what I thought. Now get on up to your place."

Pogey turned and started walking up the aisle, ending up next to Christina. He glanced at her, guilt drooping his shoulders. "Sorry."

She smiled at him. "It's okay, Pogey."

He sighed. "When are you gonna give me the rings anyway?"

"Jess has them. She'll bring them to the church tomorrow and make sure you get them."

Pogey screwed up his face, clearly trying to figure why this would be Jess's job.

"I have too much to think about tomorrow. So Jess is taking care of it for me."

"Oh."

Jess was stepping out the door. "Jess!" Pogey called.

"Yes, Pogey." She kept moving.

"Don't forget the rings. Or I'll be in big trouble."

"I'm a lawyer, boy. I forget nothin'."

That seemed to satisfy him.

Finally the rehearsal got started. Paul showed up just in time to join the other men and Jamie/Dora. Judy

149

directed them how and when to enter the church behind Paul, and where to stand.

"Okay, the music will be playin'," Judy said. "When the men are in place, the gals start. Jess first, then Maddy, Sarah, and Tanya. Come on down, walkin' easy with the music, and I'll show you each where to stand."

That part done, Judy trotted up the aisle to show Lacey and Alex how to walk down. "Slowly, okay? And you throw out the petals just a little bit at a time. Like this." She started down the aisle, pantomiming scattering the flowers. "Now you try."

The girls did their part without a hitch.

Next came Pogey, pretending like he was holding a pillow with the rings on it. Ruth watched from the front pew. At least he wasn't frowning.

Finally it was Christina's turn, carrying her paper-plate-and-bow bouquet. As she walked down the aisle — alone — Ruth studied her. She was gazing at Ben and smiling, but the smile seemed ringed with sadness. Ruth turned to look at her son. He stood with hands at his sides, fingers curling and uncurling, watching Christina with pure love on his face. Mixed into his expression was something akin to awe, as if the realization was just hitting him — *I'm really doing it. I'm really marrying this beautiful girl tomorrow.*

Tears filled Ruth's eyes. She took Sy's hand and squeezed it. He squeezed back.

Christina reached their pew, her eyes never leaving Ben's face. When she joined him up front, Judy called, "All right. Wonderful! When she gets there, y'all turn toward Paul."

Everyone started to turn — except Jess, who was staring toward the back of the church. Ruth glanced in that direction and spotted Dana Altweather, standing with hands planted on her wide hips. Dana motioned to her.

What now?

Ruth rose and hurried up the aisle. When she reached Dana, the woman led her through the vestibule and outside into the frigid air. Dana didn't seem to notice the cold. Her cheeks flamed pink, and her mouth was set tight.

Ruth shivered. "What is it?"

"I didn't want our voices to carry into the sanctuary." The police chief's wife swept back a strand of her teased hair. "I just happened to be drivin' by and saw all the cars here, which reminded me it was time for y'all's rehearsal. Then I noticed a figure loiterin' in the front"—she pointed—"half in the bushes. Made me suspicious. Stopped to check it out, and lo and behold Edna Day pops out."

"Oh, no." Ruth looked around. "Where is she?"

"I'm tellin' ya. So she takes one look at me and stops in her tracks. I says 'What're you doin' here, you're supposed to be on your way back to Texas.' She says, 'Oh, really, and what makes you think you know so much, Miss Almighty?'" Dana huffed. "She *actually* called me that. And then she says, 'What makes you think I'm supposed to be gone anyhow?'"

Dana wagged her head. "I says, 'You can't go mouthin' off to the gal at the motel desk about your so-called sufferin' at the hands of the blankety-blank Dearin's, who've turned your daughter against you and expect it to stay quiet. The Dearin's are respected in this town, and Christina's part of their family now.'"

Ruth's heart clutched. As hateful as Edna Day was acting, those words would knife right through her.

"Well that did it. She shot back a few choice words, then stomped off to her car. I watched her peel out of the parkin' lot."

Ruth's thoughts flitted over the possible consequences of the news. Clearly Edna wasn't leaving today. The sun would be setting within the half hour, and it was a good nine-hour drive to Austin. Would she insist on coming tomorrow, spewing her anger and ruining the entire wedding? Ruth could not let that happen.

Vaguely Ruth registered the sound of car engines approaching on the street.

"Have mercy, there she is now." Dana pointed.

Ruth turned to see an old red Buick with Texas plates approaching on the other side of the street. Another car was behind it. When the Buick reached even with the church, it stopped, forcing the second car to stop as well. Edna Day cranked down her window and leaned her head out. Anger creased her face.

"Looky the two town queens! Wonder what y'all are talkin' 'bout!"

The tinted window of the second car rolled down. Ruth spotted the curious face of LeAnn Hartinger, oldest checker at the grocery store and the town's second biggest gossip, next to Rita Betts.

Ruth took a few steps forward. "Edna, can we please go somewhere to talk —"

"I ain't got *nothin'* to say to *nobody* in this town." Edna lifted her chin toward Dana. "Anymore 'n' I've already said to that fat pig."

Behind her, Ruth heard the air catch in Dana's throat. LeAnn's eyes rounded. Anger swirled through Ruth. How dare Edna say something so cutting, and in front of two other people?

Edna's expression settled into smug satisfaction. "See ya 'round, y'all." She gave a little wave and drove off,

152

window still open. LeAnn gaped at Dana for a moment before driving on as well.

Ruth's throat tightened. She breathed a prayer, then turned to Dana. "I'm so sorry—"

"No need." Dana's voice pitched high with indignation and embarrassment. She knew what Ruth knew. With LeAnn as a witness, word of what Edna had called her would soon be all over town. Dana straightened her shoulders with all the dignity she could muster. "Woman's just crazy, that's all."

Ruth nodded. She wanted to say much more, but no words would form. She wanted to cry for Dana.

"Well." Dana's cheeks were pinker than ever. "I need to go now."

Ruth hugged her. "Thank you so much for stoppin' to tell me."

"Of course." Dana's words were still pinched. "That's what friends are for."

She made her way toward her car, head held high. But Ruth could feel the humiliation rolling off her stiff back.

One thing Ruth knew as she reentered the church: when Buddy Altweather heard of his beloved wife's mortification at the hands of Edna Day, he'd be looking for a reason, *anything*, to stick the woman in jail until the wedding was over. Nobody in town messed with Dana Altweather.

This meant all-out war.

CHAPTER 25

Ben drove his mom's car back to the house after the rehearsal, a silent Christina beside him. Tanya was in the back seat, staring out the window. This time Christina couldn't even cry. Neither she nor Ben knew exactly what had happened outside the church. But his mom had said all they needed to know — Edna Day was still in town and madder than ever.

Ben was back to wanting to punch his fist through a wall. The only other times he'd felt like this were when Christina had told him some new revelation of her horrendous childhood. Hadn't Edna Day done enough to her daughter in the past? Hadn't she been awful and clueless enough last night? And today at the motel? How could the woman *do* this? Ben could see no reason except for pure meanness. Edna *wanted* to destroy her daughter's wedding, that's all there was to it.

Well, it wasn't going to happen. Christina would have her beautiful wedding. She *deserved* that. And after they got back from their honeymoon, Ben would make sure Christina got a restraining order against her mother. That woman wasn't coming anywhere *near* their place of work, or their apartment, or their *lives. Ever.*

Christina sighed. "I knew she wouldn't go. It's why I let her stay last night. I should have just … left it that way."

"You did the right thing. This is her fault, not yours."

"Little good that does." Christina's breath hitched. "Now you're seeing what I've lived with all my life. If I obeyed, I lost. If I fought, I *really* lost. Nothing was in my control. Nothing." Vehemence rose in her voice. "Even now with my father gone, it's the same way. I just wanted this one day—my *wedding day*—to myself. No worrying what she would do. How she would shame me again. And now I've gone and done it. I've made her super mad, and she won't come down from that. You can bet she'll drink tonight. And probably tomorrow, right up to when she'll stagger into the wedding, and somebody'll have to drag her out. And sure, the ceremony will continue, and you and I will get married. But it was *my* day, *our* day, and we'll never get it back. And the memories will be forever stained because of *her.* Just *one. More. Thing* my parents have stolen from me."

Christina covered her face with her hands.

Ben squeezed his fingers around the steering wheel, wishing it was Edna Day's throat. "We won't let that happen, Christina. *I* won't." He exchanged a glance with Tanya through the rearview mirror. Her eyes were glistening.

At the house, Christina disappeared into the guest room. Ben let her go. She needed to pull herself together. He wanted some time of his own. He should be one hundred percent supportive of Christina, not simmering in his own anger.

He checked on Jamie, who was asleep in his bed, then sat on the floor. Leaning against a wall, he gazed around his old bedroom, remembering his childhood. True, Christina didn't have good memories of growing up. But they could create them together for their kids.

God, help us do that.

When he'd steadied himself, Ben slipped out of the room to go downstairs.

Caterers were arriving to lay out the food. His mom and sisters bustled around the kitchen, the men were in the family area, and the kids were in the play room. Ben heard all the laughter and teasing, and the usual five conversations at once. But the atmosphere felt heavy, as if a cloud hung over the house.

All because of Edna Day.

Ben curled his fingers into his palms. He felt his face tighten, the anger rush back. This had gone on long enough. Something had to be done.

He strode out of the family room, away from all the chatter. In the living room he paced, watching the floor. Thinking.

A minute later his head jerked up. He entered the kitchen and pulled his mother aside. "I need to call Buddy Altweather." He kept his voice low. "I don't know if he's on duty right now. You have his cell number?"

His mother studied him a moment, then gestured toward the family room. "My cell's on the mantel. Check my contacts."

Ben nodded his thanks. He forced himself to slow as he walked through the maze of family members in the kitchen and family room, smiling and making a comment or two. He leaned against the mantel, placing his hand over the cell phone. Then he slipped it into his pocket.

"I'm gonna check on Christina," he said to no one in particular—and left the room.

157

Outside on the porch, shivering in the chilly air, Ben found Buddy's number and dialed it from his own phone. He heard an answer on the second ring.

"Chief Altweather."

"It's Ben Dearing. I need to talk to you about Edna Day."

At the mention of the name, Ben could feel the temperature drop over the line. "I'm listenin'."

Ben began to tell the Chief his idea, but Buddy cut him off.

"Already there."

"You were thinkin' the same thing?"

"Yup. Done. I've called all four of my men, puttin' 'em on alert. We'll all be on duty tomorrow afternoon." Buddy explained his plan further, he and Ben working out the details.

Ben gazed down the road, again picturing his childhood on this street, in this town. "I just ... I can't thank you enough. And I'm really sorry for puttin' your men through all this."

"That's what we're here for." Buddy Altweather's voice edged. "Besides, it's not your doin'. That woman's caused nothin' but trouble since she set foot in Justus. Now go get married, Son. Wish I could see the weddin' with Dana." He chuckled, a grim sound. "But I got other things to do."

Ben went back into the house, the load on his shoulders lighter. The plan wasn't perfect. But it was the best he could do.

Question now was—should he tell Christina?

Minutes later she appeared, casting a worn but determined smile at everyone and receiving a lot of hugs in return. Ben watched her with a mixture of pride and love.

Tamel took Christina aside and had a few quiet words with her. Ben couldn't hear what was said, but he could imagine the context. Tamel didn't have memories of a great childhood himself, although it was nothing like Christina's. Still, he knew grief, and now he was dealing with the impending death of his father, who would likely remain crotchety and distant to his dying breath. Tamel would have to live with that.

When they finished talking Tamel gave Christina a long hug. Ben could see her mouth *Thank you.*

Maybe this wasn't the time to tell her. Maybe she'd be better off not knowing at all.

Ben's mom announced it was time to eat. With so many people to feed at once, the adults had to divide between the dining room and kitchen. But not before they all gathered in a circle and held hands for prayer. Ben's father thanked the Lord for the blessing of family and food. "And, Jesus, we ask for Your special peace on this household and weddin'. May it be a wonderful, memorable day. We also ask for restored health for Jamie. And please be with Tamel's dad. And the other folks travelin' here tonight. Amen."

Amens swept around the circle. Ben squeezed Christina's hand and whispered, "Tomorrow's our day, nobody else's. *Ours.* And it's goin' to be fine. I promise."

She smiled up at him and nodded. "*Ours.*"

159

CHAPTER 26

On Saturday morning Christina awoke before dawn.

It's my wedding day.

The amazing thought reverberated in her head—followed by the fear of what her mother would do to ruin it.

She closed her eyes and prayed that wouldn't happen, but visions of her mother, drunk and hateful, flashed through her mind. Christina clenched the bedcovers. How she wanted to be nothing but happy. Feel the excitement of this long awaited day. But already other emotions crowded in. Fear and anger. Bitterness and disappointment.

Maybe her mother had left in the night. Maybe she finally realized the terrible way she'd acted and wanted to do the right thing.

Maybe the sun wouldn't rise today.

God, please show me what to do. I need a lot of help here.

Christina showered and dressed, not stopping to put on makeup. She planned to do her own makeup and hair when it was time to get ready for the wedding.

From the kitchen filtered voices and laughter. The sounds calmed her vibrating nerves a little. No matter what happened today, she would be a part of this family. And she and Ben would be together.

By the time Christina made it to the kitchen it was nearing eight o'clock. Most of the adults were at the table, drinking coffee. Mama Ruth, Maddy, and Sarah were fixing brunch. Don, Jake, and Ben's dad were deep in conversation about golf. Everyone stopped to greet Christina with hugs and well wishes for the day. Mama Ruth laid her hands on Christina's cheeks. "You're goin' to have a lovely weddin'."

She nodded.

Sarah beamed at her. "And I'm startin' out your day by makin' you the best latte ever."

Ben was nowhere in sight. The sheet and blankets he'd used to sleep on the family room couch were still there. Lady Penelope claimed them for herself, turning around three times before lying down with a contented sigh.

"Where's Ben?" Christina took a chair at the table.

"He left to pick up Tanya." Mama Ruth stood at the counter, whisking eggs and cream in a bowl for omelets.

The unspoken words hung in the air. *At the motel. Where you mother is staying.* Christina's gaze wandered to the clock. Her mother would still be in bed at this hour, no doubt with a hangover. The wedding was at two. Maybe God would answer Christina's prayer by making her mother sleep right through it.

Uncle Keith picked up his coffee. "We should've thought to bring Tanya over from the motel."

Christina smiled at him. "She wouldn't have been ready that early anyway."

"Right-oh. We were hot to trot, countin' on that free breakfast you got goin' over there. Right, Ruthie?"

"You bet."

Uncle Keith looked back to Christina. "By the way, I thought the bride's not supposed to see the groom before the weddin' on the day thereof."

"Little hard when they're stayin' in the same house," Aunt Dora said.

"Oh. I thought it was a rule."

"Weddin's have no rules. They're whatever you want 'em to be. All formal and hoity-toity, or casual."

"What about the weddin' gown, has Ben seen that?"

"No way." Christina shook her head. "You have to have *some* surprises."

"I thought there are no rules."

"Well, that's *my* rule."

"Oh. Got it."

Aunt Dora popped a chocolate espresso bean in her mouth. "However you plan the weddin'"—she sucked on the bean—"main thing is there's love and family around."

"Here, here." Ben's dad raised his mug. "And we got plenty of that."

Uncle Keith leaned toward his wife. "Don't you go eatin' too many of those, woman. You already talk enough."

She elbowed him in the ribs.

"What about bachelor and bachelorette parties, did you do that?" Uncle Keith asked Christina.

"Yes, in Dallas. Last weekend."

"Have a good time?"

Christina pictured her friends chattering away in the restaurant's private room, with nothing but excitement for Christina and the wedding. No worries of what her mother might do. That's how this weekend was supposed to be. And if they hadn't needed to move the wedding outside of Texas—because of her mother—all those friends would be with her today.

"It was really nice."

Christina heard the garage door open. *Ben and Tanya.* She jumped up and greeted them when they stepped into the hall.

Tanya studied her. "How're you doing?"

"Okay. Where's your dress and everything?"

"In the car."

"Hello, beautiful." Ben hugged Christina, his boyish face full of anticipation. "You ready for our day?"

Christina lowered her voice. "Did you see her?"

He shook his head. "Her car's there, though."

The tiny hope that her mother had miraculously left in the night trickled away.

"Don't worry, it'll be okay." Ben brushed hair off Christina's forehead. "Nothin's gonna spoil our weddin'. And in just a few hours you'll be Christina Dearing."

He looked so excited, as they both should be. She had no right to bring him down. "I can't believe it."

"Me either." He looked at Tanya and frowned. "I don't know, though. I've been thinkin'—maybe we oughtta put this thing off."

Tanya smacked him on the arm. Ben grinned.

"Your latte's done, Christina!" Sarah called.

"Thanks, coming!"

Tanya went on into the kitchen. Ben held Christina's arm, urging her to stay. She heard Mama Ruth invite Tanya to sit down for breakfast.

"Look," Ben said. "I don't think your mom's gonna show up. It'll be okay, really, I just feel it. And even if she does, she'll probably just slip into the back and watch. That won't hurt anything."

164

Oh, Ben. His positivity could be downright naïve at times. "If that's all she'd do, you're right. But that's not what she wants. She wants to be *part* of the wedding, recognized as the bride's mother. Plus, now she's so mad I've told her to leave, no telling what tricks she'll pull. And she won't be sober."

"So what should we do?"

Christina had no clue. Should she keep fighting, knowing that wouldn't work? Or should she just let her mother roll all over her, like she'd done her entire childhood? "I don't *know*."

Ben put his hands on her shoulders. "Okay. Just ... don't worry about it."

"How am I not supposed to worry about it?" Christina's eyes grew moist.

"See? That's exactly what I *don't* want you doin' on our weddin' day. She has no right to steal your happiness. I *will not* let her."

Christina looked down and nodded.

"Listen." Ben pushed up her chin with two fingers. "You really don't need to worry because I've taken care of it."

"What do you mean?"

Ben firmed his mouth. "I talked to Buddy Altweather yesterday—our police chief. He and his four men are stationin' themselves around the church, at every intersection she might have to drive through to get there."

Christina's jaw unhinged. "You're kidding me."

"No. They want to help. They and everybody else in Justus want you to have your weddin'."

They would do this for *her*? She hardly knew these people. "You mean it's for you."

"For *both* of us. The women at your shower all loved you."

And Dana Altweather had been one of them.

Relief wafted through Christina, only to spritz away. "She *will* try to come. You know she will."

"She's not invited. They're gonna ask to see her invitation, and when she can't show it, they'll stop her."

What? "Nobody else has to show an invitation."

"Nobody else is Edna Day."

Christina put a hand to her mouth. Should she laugh or cry? She couldn't believe this would really keep her mother away. The woman hadn't been invited to the shower either, yet she'd managed to find out where it was—two states away—and show up. Plus, her mother had a nose for cops. She'd likely spot them and sneak in on foot. Madder than ever.

"So if she tries to come, Christina, they'll take care of it. I *don't* want you worryin' any more."

This would not stop her from worrying, no way. She'd only do it all the more. But Ben was trying so hard to protect her.

"Okay?"

Christina nodded. "Okay."

Ben smiled. "You go on back to the kitchen now. I'm gonna check on Jamie."

Christina returned to her seat and tried to calm her shaky nerves with the latte.

When Ben returned he brought a pale Jamie with him. Jamie's brown hair was tousled, and his eyes were at half mast. "Hi, everybody." He shoved his hands in his jeans pockets. "Sorry I was so ... out of it last night."

"Jamie, so glad you're feelin' better!" Mama Ruth walked over to him. "Come meet everyone and grab a seat at the table. Can you eat? You should have at least a little somethin'."

"Maybe some toast."

"Oh, good. If you can manage anything more, we've got plenty. We're havin' a large brunch since there'll be

166

no time to cook at noon." Mama Ruth motioned toward the table. "Just kick someone off if you have to."

"Take my chair, I'll fetch another one." Ben's father rose and held out his hand to Jamie. "Syton Dearing. Good to have you with us."

"Thank you, sir. Appreciate your hospitality."

Jake and Don stood to introduce themselves, as did Uncle Keith. "And this one here's Dora." Uncle Keith indicated his wife. "She belongs to me — "

"*You* belong to *me*, and don't you forget it." Aunt Dora pointed at him.

" — And that's Maddy over there, who belongs to Don. I mean, Don belongs to her. And that's Sarah. She's with Jake. Or he's with her. Or somethin' like that."

Jamie looked around the group with a bemused smile.

"Where are the kids?" Tanya asked.

"Still in bed." Sarah dropped thick slices of homemade bread into the toaster.

Ben sat next to Christina, laying a hand on her knee. Sudden butterflies flitted through her stomach. Tonight they would be on their honeymoon, starting in a hotel in Jackson. Tomorrow they'd fly to Cabo San Lucas. They'd be together for a whole week. *Alone.* After that they'd have years to build their lives.

Years.

Her mother couldn't stop any of that. No matter how hard she tried.

Jess puffed into the kitchen, wearing a running suit and knit hat, her cheeks red.

"Hey, Jess." Aunt Dora looked her up and down. "I thought you were still in bed."

"Shoot, no." Jess grabbed a glass from the cabinet. "I've already run four miles while y'all sat here on your butts."

"Careful talkin' 'bout butts now," Don said.

167

"Yeah, not allowed on the day of a weddin'." Ben's dad wagged a finger.

"Or any other day," Aunt Dora declared.

The brunch was served—cheese and bacon omelets, small red roasted potatoes, and toast. It smelled wonderful, even though Christina couldn't eat much. As the food was passed around, she managed to smile at everyone's jokes, feeling Ben's nearness and the love of family. It all seemed surreal. The day she'd dreamed about since a child was *here.*

And so was her mother.

By nine-thirty everyone was stuffed. Most of the men had scattered, and the kids were having their turn at the breakfast table. Uncle Keith and Aunt Dora had gone back to their motel room. Pogey was moaning about wearing his tux, and the little girls were chattering about their pretty matching red dresses. Jess had answered a call from Tamel and wandered out of the kitchen to talk.

Time to start getting ready.

Christina's insides trembled. She would do her makeup and hair here, as would the bridesmaids. Then they and the flower girls would all go to the church at noon to get dressed. The men would dress at the house. At twelve-thirty the photographer would begin taking pictures of Christina and her attendants. The men had to be at the church at one o'clock for their photos. Pictures of the entire wedding party would be done immediately after the ceremony.

Christina kissed Ben on the cheek. "'Bye."

"What do you mean 'bye?"

As if he didn't know.

"Time for me to get ready. At this point you can't see me again until the wedding."

"Not at all?"

"Nope."

168

"You mean the next time I see you, you'll be walkin' down the aisle and into my arms?"

Christina's throat constricted. She gave him a shaky smile. "That's exactly what I mean."

CHAPTER 27

The clock in the master bedroom read ten-forty-five. Even in her own room with the door closed Ruth could feel the excitement and tension swirling through the house. At this point every minute needed to go as planned. Family had been fed and the kitchen was clean. Time to check on the flowers.

But first—another quick prayer.

Ruth sat on the edge of her bed and closed her eyes. "Jesus," she spoke aloud, "here I am again, askin' for help through this day. I know You work in mysterious ways. I know You are a God of healin' and want to see the relationship between Christina and her mother restored. It's so bad, Lord, only You could do that. But today's the weddin'. Christina and Ben have looked forward to this day for months, and now Edna could ruin it. Please don't let her do that. Whatever it takes, Lord, just do ... *somethin'*. But Your will be done. If somethin' does happen, please help us get through it. Amen."

Ruth opened her eyes and sighed. Sometimes God answered prayer with an absolute *Yes*. Sometimes with a *No*. But so many times the answer was in between, the *Yes* coming in an unexpected way or much later than hoped. Or the *No* leading to a different blessing altogether. The Lord was certainly full of creativity.

Ten-fifty. Time was ticking. Ruth picked up the phone and dialed Judy Crenshaw's cell. Judy would be at the church by now, receiving the flower order. The line barely rang before she answered.

"Hey, Ruthie, you hangin' in there on this big day?"

"Yup. The flowers there?"

"All arrived. I counted each one. They're lovely. The red roses will look stunnin' against that white and black gown. Then we have the white roses for the other gals, and all the men's boutonnieres, and your corsage."

"Wonderful. And flowers for the reception tables?"

"The florist is settin' them up now. They've already draped the hall with those long, white gauzy pieces you and Christina chose, plus the glittery fabric streamers. I'm tellin' you, the place just looks *beautiful*."

That had been Christina's idea—an inexpensive way to transform a church gathering hall into something elegant. The girl had worked *so hard* planning for this special day. "I'm so glad."

"Plus all the sanctuary arrangements are here, so all's ready. I'll see y'all here at noon."

"Any sign of Edna?"

"No."

Not that this meant anything. There would be little reason for her to show up early. Edna Day seemed to enjoy making an entrance.

Ruth shivered.

"All right, thanks. If you see her, give me a call, okay?"

172

"Will do."

Ruth ended the call and rose to put on her makeup and do her hair. She planned to be ready early just in case … who knew what.

A pounding came from the bedroom door. "Mama!" Jess's voice.

"What? Come in."

The door flew open. Jess hurried in, clad in a bathrobe, her blonde hair still wet from a shower. A cell phone was in her hand. "Henry Curd's bein' rushed to the hospital, and Tamel's goin' in the ambulance. He's not sure he can make the weddin'."

CHAPTER 28

Tamel perched on a seat in the back of the speeding ambulance, feeling the sway as they rounded bends in the road. The siren *whop-whopped*, sending chills through his veins. Less than an hour ago Henry Curd had woken from a nap, barely able to breathe. Tamel called 911. The medics who arrived said fluid from the man's legs had flowed to the lungs. Hadn't been the first time. One of them immediately administered an IV with Lasix to ease off the fluid. His father was now sitting up, still fighting for breath, gray-faced beneath an oxygen mask. The medic was setting up leads on his chest for an EKG.

Tamel reached out and ran a finger along his father's hand. It was cold

Like his father had always been.

This could be it—the end of the drawn-out demise of heart failure. Numerous times they'd brought Henry Curd back from the brink with Lasix. But today it was worse, and his father had little strength left. Still he clung to life. He'd never signed a do not resuscitate form—hadn't wanted anything to do with it. Stubborn Henry Curd would fight to the end.

Watching him now, Tamel did not begin to know how to feel.

He checked his watch. Eleven-ten. He needed to be at the church at one o'clock for pictures. He wasn't even dressed yet. The hospital was twenty-five minutes from his house. He'd have little time to assess the situation once they arrived. If he could leave for the wedding, he'd have to call a cab and hope it showed up in a hurry.

The medic started running the EKG.

As much as Tamel had worked to prepare himself for his father's death, he wasn't ready for it. Nothing had changed between them, no matter how hard he'd tried. No supportive words from Henry Curd—*Thank you. I love you. I'm proud of you.* Did he truly not care about connecting with his son before he died? Or did he simply not know how?

And now it might be too late.

Pain coursed through Tamel, sizzling like acid. He closed his eyes.

The medic read the EKG results over the phone to a doctor at the hospital. Tamel heard the words "A-fib."

The ambulance slowed. They'd reached the outskirts of Jacksonville.

"Five more minutes," the medic said.

Tamel nodded.

The ambulance soon stopped, its siren dying with a wail. The doors flew open, cold December air flowing in. The driver appeared, and the two medics quickly transferred Tamel's father out. They headed for the hospital doors. Tamel followed on legs he did not quite feel, the sanitized, brightly lit walls of the emergency room flowing past. At the door to a room, a nurse stopped him. She looked in her sixties, with graying hair and a plump face that spoke of seeing more than her share of family trauma.

"You'll need to wait outside now, okay?" Her words were compassionate but firm. "We'll let you know as soon as we find out anything."

Tamel watched a doctor push his father inside, the nurse following. Would it be the last time he saw his father alive?

He focused on Henry Curd's face until he could see it no more.

The door closed behind them.

Sudden quiet descended on the corridor. Tamel leaned against the wall, rushed by memories of his mother's death so many years ago. She'd been his world, his rock. One of his worst memories was going home from her funeral with his stone-faced father only to wander around the house with no clue what to do next, how to live.

Thank God for the Dearings, who became his second family. Mama Ruth fed him countless suppers over the years. And somewhere along the way he'd fallen in love with Jessica, with all her passion and wild independence. She drove him crazy half the time.

Tamel would not, *could* not live without her.

He paced the hall. The minutes ticked by like days.

The next time he checked his watch it read twelve o'clock. They'd been working on his father for half an hour.

From inside his pocket, his cell phone vibrated. Tamel pulled it out and saw Jess's picture on the screen. "Hi."

"How is he?"

"Not good. But I don't know anything yet."

Silence. Tamel could feel the mix of emotions pulsing between them.

"I'm so sorry, Tamel. I wanted to come after you. But I was just gettin' out of the shower when you called."

"I know. You're fine. You're where you need to be."

"I want to be with you."

The words brought tears to Tamel's eyes.

Movement down the corridor caught his attention. Tamel turned his head to see the nurse motioning to him. His heart stilled. "Gotta go. Call you back soon."

He clicked off the line and stuffed the phone in his pocket, already moving toward his father's room.

CHAPTER 29

At noon Ben jerked open the refrigerator door and scanned the shelves for leftovers. What was the matter with him? He'd eaten a huge brunch just three hours before, but he was *starving*. Had to be nerves. And Ben wasn't used to being nervous. No reason why he should be now. Just because he was getting married in two hours—and his best man was back in bed, still shaky from food poisoning. And now another groomsman may not be there at all because his father was dying. Poor Tamel. Ben couldn't imagine facing that. *And* of course there was his future monster-in-law, who'd likely ruin whatever was left of the ceremony.

Ben grabbed a plastic container of roasted potatoes and shoved it in the microwave to nuke. Carcinogenic or not, he had no time to dump them in a plate.

He heated them only halfway through and stood at the counter, gulping them down.

How was Christina? He wished he could check on her, but she was at the church now with the other women. Besides, when he'd tried before it hadn't done any good. Ben had knocked on her bedroom door just before they left. Tanya answered and told him to go away.

"But I just wanna—"

"Ben. She's fine. She's getting ready."

"How can she be fine?"

Tanya gave him a scorching look. "You want to make her all the more nervous?"

"I … no."

"Then go away." The door slammed.

When they left the house Ben had been ordered to stay in the kitchen where he couldn't see Christina. Tanya hauled out Christina's suitcase for Ben to put in his mom's car. After the wedding and reception he and Christina would be leaving straight from the church for their hotel in Jackson. Tomorrow someone would drive Ben's mom to get her car and take them to the airport for their flight to Cabo. So many details.

Ben had made Tanya promise she'd call if they saw any sign of Edna Day around the church. If that happened Ben would be there in a heartbeat.

He ate the last potato and chucked the plastic container and fork into the sink.

Quiet footsteps sounded from the family room. Ben turned to see Pogey sauntering toward the kitchen table, one hand behind his back.

They eyed each other.

"What's up, Pogey?"

"Nothin'."

The thing about Pogey—every emotion showed in his round freckled face. And right now it was covered in guilt.

"What're you doin' in here?"

"Um. Just wanted to pet Penny."

"Penny's behind you in her bed."

"Oh. Yeah." Pogey started to back up.

"Hey. Nephew. What're you hidin' in your hand there?"

"Nothin'."

"Uh-huh." Ben strode over and pulled Pogey's hand out from behind his back. A small plastic bag dangled from his fingers. Ben took the bag and held it up. Stared at it.

A light dawned.

"Don't tell me you ate any of these."

"Well, I just ... See, Aunt Dora left them on the table when they went back to the motel, so I figured I'd take 'em to her at the weddin' — "

"Pogey. *How many* did you eat?"

The boy's face flushed. "One."

No way. "One?"

"Maybe two?"

Ben grabbed his wrist. "How many?"

Pogey looked at his shoes. "I dunno, maybe ten."

"*Ten?* Are you kiddin' me?"

His nephew cringed. "They're just candy."

"They are *not* just candy! You've probably just ingested the equivalent of who knows how many cups of coffee!"

"I thought they were chocolate."

"You *knew* they weren't just chocolate. Your mama told you to stay away from 'em."

Pogey ran his tongue under his top lip. "Sorry."

"Uh-huh. It's a little late for that." Oh, man. This was just ... "You might be feelin' even sorrier in a minute."

181

Ben turned on his heel and headed down the hall to Sarah's old room. He banged on the door. It swung back to reveal Jake, shirtless and wearing his tuxedo pants.

"What is it?"

"Your son just ate ten of Dora's extra-caffeinated chocolate-covered beans."

Jake's eyes widened.

"He's likely to be bouncin' off walls by the weddin'."

"I'm *fine*." Pogey's voice came from behind Ben. "I don't feel nothin'."

Ben pushed his nephew forward none too gently. "Go on, your father can deal with you. And it's time to get dressed. We gotta be at the church in less than an hour."

As he stomped away, he heard Jake's angry voice. "Boy, you are in *so much* trouble."

The door banged shut.

Ben took the stairs to his bedroom two steps at a time. He needed to finish packing for his honeymoon and get dressed himself—not to mention check on Jamie, who may or may not be his best man in two hours.

CHAPTER 30

"Oh, that's beautiful." The photographer aimed her camera at Christina, its shutter clicking. "Now move your head a little bit so we'll get some different angles."

Christina obeyed, smiling, smiling. While inside she thought her lungs would explode.

She stood before an array of flowers set up as a beautiful background for close-ups. When pictures were done the arrangements would be moved to the sanctuary. They'd been able to start the photos fifteen minutes early. With everything going on, they might need the extra time. After the ceremony, pictures of the wedding party would be taken in the sanctuary.

The flower girls, Mama Ruth, and all Christina's bridesmaids except Jess looked on from across the room, along with Judy Crenshaw. The attendants looked so pretty in their red dresses. Mama Ruth wore a lovely light green that made her brown hair and soft skin come alive. Lacey and Alex couldn't stop looking at themselves in the full-length mirror. Everyone's hair was curled and adorned with white flowers to match their bouquets. They all were everything Christina had imagined—and more.

But the worry biting her insides would not let up.

Phone calls had gone back and forth, someone's cell ringing every few minutes with a new update. Still she had no final word. How was Henry Curd? Would Tamel make it to the wedding? If he didn't, Jess would lose her escort. What about Jamie, could he pull himself out of bed? And Jess needed to be here any minute. She'd been delayed getting ready because of Tamel's news.

Most of all—*where* was her mother?

Christina's heart *rat-tatted*. She smiled some more, turning her head this way and that for different poses.

"Wonderful." Sheila Adley lowered her camera. The middle-aged woman's cheeks shone from the passion of her work. "Honestly, I've never seen a more beautiful bride."

"She's right, Christina." Sarah smiled at her. "You're incredibly gorgeous."

"Thank you."

Sheila backed up. "Okay, now let's get your full body shots. Tanya and Judy, want to help arrange her gown and veil?"

Christina stood, feeling the weight of the floor-length veil pulling at the crown of her head. She looked down at the black-on-white designs on her dress as Tanya and Miss Judy arranged the full skirt to perfection. A wave of disbelief crashed over Christina. Despite all of the unknowns around her, despite even her mother, this was her *wedding day*. She was actually here, in the gown she'd so carefully chosen, with her new family around her. In a little over an hour she'd walk down the aisle toward Ben—the man who'd put a face to her desperate childhood dreams of love.

This was really *happening.*

Christina felt her cheeks flush. She looked at Mama Ruth and her new sisters and nieces, tears threatening her eyes. *No, no,* she couldn't cry—not now in all her makeup.

"Thank you." She focused on Sarah first, then the others. "All of you. You have no idea ..." The tears thickened. "Oh." She flapped her hand. "I need a tissue."

Miss Judy pushed one into her fingers. "Dab gently. And no worries, happens to brides all the time."

Maybe so. Christina held the tissue to her eyes to absorb the moisture. But not like this. Never quite like *this.*

Sheila studied Christina's gown. "Okay, that looks great. Ready for some more pictures, lovely lady?"

Christina nodded.

"Let's practice walkin' down the aisle." Alex poked Lacey. "Mama, we want our flowers."

The baskets full of petals were sitting on a table against the wall, along with the bridesmaids' bouquets, a jumble of toiletries, and bottles of water.

"I told you, Alex." Maddy shook her head. "You can't have 'em until it's time for the weddin'."

Alex stuck out her lip. "I want mine *now.*"

Lacey regarded her cousin with all the wisdom of an extra year of life. "Well, you'll just have to wait."

"Fine then. I'm *not* practicin'." Alex flounced away toward the corner of the room. For a moment Christina thought she'd stick her nose against the wall and hunch her back, just like Lady Penelope.

"All right, Christina." Sheila readied her camera. "Look this way."

"Alex." Maddy's voice was sharp. "You want some of that weddin' cake you been talkin' about?"

"Yes."

"Then button your lip or you're not gettin' any."

185

"Christina." Sheila waved at her. "Over here."

"Everybody be quiet," Sarah said. "Let her concentrate."

Christina smiled and posed while the shutter clicked.

Her cell rang. Christina jumped.

"Can somebody get that?" Sheila looked to Mama Ruth. "I don't want her movin' right now."

Christina tensed as she watched Mama Ruth pick up her phone and check the screen.

"Hi, Ben."

Every pair of eyes in the room fastened on Mama Ruth. Her eyebrows rose. She looked to Christina with an encouraging nod. "Okay. Thanks." She ended the call. "Jamie's up and dressed. He and all the men at the house are on their way."

Relieved murmurs went around the room. Christina breathed a quick prayer of thanks.

"That's one down." Sarah held up her forefinger.

"What about Tamel?" Christina asked.

"No word yet. But we'll hear soon." Mama Ruth shot her a reassuring smile.

Christina checked the clock on the far wall. Twelve-thirty. If Tamel hadn't left the hospital yet, he'd be late for the men's pictures.

"Okay, let's keep movin'." Sheila edged a little closer to Christina. "Almost done here, and then we can get the flower girls."

"Hear that, Alex?" Maddy said. "Better straighten up or your pictures are gonna look all scowly."

Alex's bottom lip looked fatter than ever.

Just as Sheila finished Christina's full-length pictures, the door banged open and Jess hurried inside. Her blonde hair was curled, and her makeup was perfect beneath her flushed cheeks.

"Sorry I'm late. And Tamel's comin'. I just called Ben."

Fresh relief flooded Christina.

"Oh, thank God." Mama Ruth laced her hands and brought them to her chin.

"Well, hallelujah!" Judy Crenshaw looked heavenward. "We got the whole weddin' party."

Jess pulled up in front of Christina, breathless. "So sorry I'm late."

"Don't worry about that." Christina touched her arm. "How's Tamel's father?"

"Stable for the moment. The doctors told Tamel he's not goin' to die today. The final signs aren't there yet. But they think it may come in the next few days. At this point there's really nothin' more they can do."

The room grew still.

"Poor Tamel," Christina whispered. "I just can't imagine ..."

Jess nodded. "I know. But he's okay. I've been on the phone with him on and off. He really doesn't want to miss the weddin'."

"That's ... so good of him."

They exchanged a sad smile.

Jess straightened. "Okay." She looked around the room. "So no more worries, everyone, it's almost time for a weddin'! Have I held up pictures?"

No more worries? Christina bit her lip. Except for the biggest one of all—her mother. She exchanged a look with Jess—and knew Jess was thinking the same thing.

"No, you're fine," Judy said. "They're just gettin' to the flower girls."

"Long as Alex stops poutin'." Maddy aimed a hard look at her daughter. "You want to be in this weddin' or not?"

Alex stuck her hands on her hips. "Yes!"

"Then start grinnin' like the Cheshire Cat. Now."

"Whoa." Jess raised her eyebrows at Sarah. "What do you know—Maddy actually got a sayin' right."

Sarah wagged her head. "You sure you don't mean 'like the Cheshire Dog', Maddy?"

Jess laughed. "Or maybe the cat that sang like a canary?"

"Oh, will you two knock it off!" Maddy turned back to Alex, who had her chin raised, face muscles clearly fighting to morph a frown into a smile. Maddy shook her head. "Work a little faster."

The pixie face slowly brightened into a smile.

"That's it. Now go over there and get your picture taken before you lose it." Maddy pushed Alex toward Sheila.

"And I'll get your baskets just for this part, girls." Judy headed toward the table holding all the flowers. Alex let out a happy squeal.

Christina moved aside while Sheila concentrated on the girls' photos. Christina's feet were already tired, but it was hard to sit in the gown. Her eyes wandered back to the clock. Twelve-forty-five. She'd be *getting married* in an hour and fifteen minutes.

Disbelief tingled her veins.

From that moment time blurred as the photographs continued. The bridesmaids individually and together. Then with the bride. Followed by all the women. Pictures of Mama Ruth alone. Then with Christina. And her daughters. All together in various poses. Lips curved, and the shutter clicked, and nervous energy swirled. Christina did her best to push down her clawing anxiety—to no avail. By the time they were done, it was twenty minutes after one—far later than they'd expected.

"Okay, that's a wrap." Sheila checked over her camera. "I've got to go photograph the men."

Exhaustion weighted Christina's lungs. In the sudden lull the fear over her mother made her light-headed. She put a hand to her forehead. "I have to sit down."

"I'll help you with the gown." Tanya stepped to her side. With some careful maneuvering Christina settled into a chair.

"You should drink some water." Mama Ruth fetched her a bottle from the table.

Jess couldn't seem to hold still. She paced the room, then focused on her watch. Her head jerked up. "Tamel should be here by now. I'm gonna go check on him."

"They'll be busy with pictures." Sarah patted one of Lacey's curls back into place.

"I just have to make sure he's okay." Jess was already headed for the door.

"*Wait!*" Christina called.

Jess veered toward her. "What? You okay?"

"I ..." Christina glanced at Alex and Lacey. She lowered her voice. "When you came in ... did you see the policemen around?"

Jess gave her a grim smile. "They're out there." She leaned down to squeeze Christina's hand. "It's gonna be okay. They won't let her through."

Christina held her eyes, then nodded. If only she could believe that.

Jess straightened. "I'm gonna go see Tamel, okay? Be right back."

"Okay."

Jess hurried out of the room.

Maddy and Sarah exchanged a look. Sarah swung her head back and forth. "She doesn't love that man, not at all."

"Goodness no. She's far too independent for that."

Mama Ruth smiled but said nothing.

Christina took a drink of water and closed her eyes. *Breathe in. Breathe out.* Part of her wanted to run outside, look up and down the street. *Where* was her mother? How drunk was she?

And what would she do when she got inside the church?

CHAPTER 31

Ben posed in front of Sheila's camera, trying hard to relax. Not that anyone else was making it easy. Caffeine-crazed Pogey had taken over one side of the room, fighting imaginary opponents with wild Ninja kicks and arm thrusts. His tux was creasing, and his bow tie had long gone crooked. With every movement he let out a "Hee! Whaaa!" Jake could not shut him up. If you tied the kid with ropes, he'd ricochet right out of them. Tamel was walking the floor, obviously too wound up over his father to sit, even as he'd smiled and back-slapped Ben in congratulations. Jamie sat with his head against the wall, pasty-faced but determined to stand through the wedding.

Don and Ben's dad might be the only normal ones in the room right now—if they'd just quit counting down Ben's remaining minutes of being a free man.

And how was Christina?

And what was Edna Day doing?

Ben's palms were sweaty.

"All right, handsome groom, smile for me." Sheila aimed her camera.

"He sure *is* handsome." Ben's dad gave him a thumbs up.

Ben curved his mouth.

Jess materialized in the doorway, stunning in her red dress and curled hair.

"Whoo-whoo," whistled Don, "check out Jessica."

She peered around the room. "Same to ya, boys."

Tamel gazed at her, the expression on his face tugging at Ben's heart. "Hi."

Jess headed straight for him, casting sideways glances at Pogey. "Might want to kick a little higher there, boy, looks like you're runnin' outta steam."

Ben rolled his eyes. "Don't encourage him." The shutter clicked while his mouth was open. "Oh, sorry."

Jess and Tamel met in the middle of the room, their conversation in low tones. Ben heard snatches of it amidst Sheila's instructions. "... see how you're doin'." "You look incredible." "So do you."

Pose and click, pose and click. Ben would be so glad when this part was over.

"All right, Ben, that's good." Sheila lowered her camera. "How about we do the ring bearer now?"

"Hey, Son!" Jake's voice was sharp. "Stop fightin' and start smilin'."

Pogey aimed a kick so high the force knocked him on his rear end. "Woooo!" He raised victorious hands in the air.

"Pogey." Jake strode over and jerked him up. "Come on, man, pull it together. Let's see you smile."

Pogey's lips spread in a rictus grin, his eyebrows practically disappearing into his hairline.

"Hahaha!" Don bent over, laughing. "Jack Nicholson in *The Shining.*"

Ben's dad tried to keep a straight face. His blue eyes sparkled.

"All right, Pogey, come over here." Sheila beckoned him. "Where's your pillow and rings? We'll do a few shots with them."

"Pillow's over there." Pogey ran to a chair to fetch the puffy white rectangle. "Aunt Jess has the rings."

Jess swiveled toward Pogey. Her mouth opened into a large O.

Oh, no. No, no, no. "Jess." Ben's heart stilled. "Tell me you brought the rings."

She cringed. "Maybe … not."

"You told me you never forget anything!" Pogey shot her an indignant look. "Now I can't do my job."

"I just … with Tamel's dad and everything …"

"Jess, I'm gettin' married in half an hour!" Ben spread his hands. What *else* could go wrong?

"Yeah, well, the house is five minutes away." Jess made for the door, a woman on a mission. "I just gotta get the house keys from Mama."

"Hurry!" Ben dropped into a chair beside Jamie. He could not believe this. She'd probably have a car accident on the way back. Or something. This wedding would *never* happen.

"No pictures now?" Pogey aimed the question at Sheila, bouncing on his toes.

"Pictures now. We'll do the pillow later." Sheila looked all business. "Come on, men, we're runnin' out of time here."

And Ben was about to run out of sanity.

CHAPTER 32

Jess carved to a stop in front of her parents' house. Every vein in her body zinged, and a headache had set in. How in the world could she have done this! She shoved open the door and ran as fast as her heels would allow up the sidewalk, keys dangling from her hand. Cold air nipped through the thin sleeves of her dress, but she barely noticed.

When she reached the porch she heard a strange sound. Penny barking in a total frenzy.

For a second Jess slowed, listening. She happened to glance down the road—and spotted a red Buick parked some distance away. It had Texas plates.

What?

Jess flew up the steps and to the front door. Started to slide her key into the lock—but the knob turned in her hand. Had Edna Day broken into the *house*?

She shoved the door open and jumped inside.

Penny's insistent barking was coming from behind the family room pocket door, which had been pulled shut.

On impulse Jess veered left through the living and dining room. The pocket door leading into the kitchen was closed, too. No wonder Penny was so ticked.

Jess pushed back the door and called through the kitchen. "Penny, this way!"

The barking stopped. Lady Penelope came tearing toward Jess and through the doorway. She raced through the dining room and took the corner into the living room at top speed. As Jess followed, Penny skidded around the corner into the hallway. Little thuds sounded as she took the stairs.

Jess ran back through the living room and started up the steps. If she caught Edna Day up there she would go ballistic.

Penny careened into Jess's bedroom and broke into more manic barking. The sound cut through Jess's head.

"Penny, knock it *off!*" She ran into the room—and saw a leg dangling from the ceiling.

Jess skidded to a halt, an ankle turning in its high heel. "Ow!"

Arms frozen midair, she ogled the rest of the scene. Plaster on the carpet. The pull down stairs to the attic— open. A purse and a pair of black stilettoes nearby. Attic light on. Penny at the bottom, pitchin' a fit.

Jess kicked off her shoes. She planted her feet wide apart and stared openmouthed at the leg. It hung about six feet away from the attic opening, ending at the thigh. Bare foot. Skin-tight black pants. Coated in bits of plaster and dust.

It could only belong to Edna Day.

The leg swung back and forth, sending out puffs of white. "Somebody there? Helllp!" Edna's throaty voice, slurry with alcohol, filtered down the stairs.

Jess blinked upward. *What in the —*

Lady Penelope barked all the louder.

"Penny, shut *up*!" Jess scooped the dog into her arms, but the yapping continued. The sound cut through Jess's head. She hurried back to the hall, favoring her hurt ankle, and put Penny down none too gently. Slammed the door in the Yorkie's face. Penny kept barking, but at least Jess could *think*.

"Helllp!"

Jess turned around and focused on the waving leg, her eyes narrowing. How *dare* Edna Day invade her bedroom. Not to mention fall through her ceiling. Jess planted her hands on her hips.

"*What* are you *doin'* up there?"

Silence. The leg froze.

"Edna!"

"Gemme out."

"What are you *doin'* here?" Jess stalked to the bottom of the stairs, ignoring the pain in her ankle.

"I just … Gemme down!"

"You sure you want to get down? 'Cause then you're gonna have to face me."

"I ain't scared a you."

Drunken witch *should* be. "Get down yourself!"

"I can't."

"What do you mean you can't?"

"I'm stuck."

Jess drew back her head. *Huh?* She studied the top of Edna's leg as it disappeared. In a flash it hit her. Stupid woman had stepped off the attic flooring onto the pink insulation, the plaster of the ceiling not enough to hold her weight. And sure enough what remained around her leg looked plenty tight.

"Get me *dowwwwn*. Come on."

The wedding was about to start—and Edna Day was *caught in her ceiling*? A laugh spurted from Jess.

"Don't you *dare* make fun a me!" Edna's voice turned to venom.

"Easy for you to say. You should see the view from here."

From the hall, Lady Penelope kept up her barking. The dog was going to end up with one mighty sore throat.

Jess checked her watch. Eighteen minutes before two. She had to get out of here.

She pulled herself up the ladder, wincing at her ankle, until her line of sight cleared the attic opening. To her right Edna Day splayed awkwardly under the slanted roof, one leg on the flooring with knee bent, the other gone. She wore a plunging neckline—naturally—this time on a tight red sweater. The sloppy ice-scowl on her painted face could have sunk the Titanic.

"*Don't* you laugh at me."

Jess lowered her chin. "You got no right tellin' me what to do when you're stuck in my ceilin'. Which, by the way, is gonna cost good money to fix."

"You think I meant to fall through it?"

"*What* are you doin' here?"

Edna swung her head away. "I was lookin' for pictures, if you have to know."

"Pictures. Do tell."

"For that." Edna waved a hand toward the other side of the opening.

Jess swiveled her head. On the attic floor lay a large black frame with six matted areas for photos. Three were filled. Jess leaned toward the frame, squinting. They were of Christina as a child.

She looked back to Edna. "You were lookin' for old pictures of Christina—*here*?"

Edna flicked her eyes toward the roof. "No, stupid. Of Ben."

Jess's veins sizzled. "You're in a fine state to call *me* stupid."

Edna huffed.

"So let me get this straight. You broke into our house—"

"I didn't break in, it wasn't locked."

"And—"

"I figured it wouldn't be, what with everybody hurryin' out for the weddin'." At the last word, Edna's voice caught.

Jess stared at her.

Edna firmed her mouth and looked Jess in the eye. "It's my weddin' present, don't I have a right to give one? To *my* daughter. Pictures of her and the man she loves. From when they were kids like"—Edna's gaze dropped—"like they were meant to be together. From way back."

Jess couldn't find a response.

Edna shot her another defiant look. "I meant to ask your mama for the pictures right from the start. But then I got here, and she and all y'all treated me like dirt—"

"My mother did *not* treat you like dirt! She tried to be nice. *You* walked in our front door crazy—and you haven't stopped bein' crazy ever since!"

Edna's face reddened. "How crazy would *you* be if other people stole your daughter?"

"We didn't—." Jess's words cut off. What was the point in arguing with a woman who refused to hear?

"You did, you *stole* her from meeeee." Out of nowhere, Edna heaved into drunken sobs. The tears ran black from her heavy mascara, smearing down her face. "She's the only thing I had l-left in this w-world."

Jess gaped at her.

199

Edna cried for another minute then straightened, her expression turning dark. "All I wanted was to come to my daughter's weddin'."

"Dressed like that?" Jess pointed to her sweater.

Edna had the gall to look offended. "'Course not. I was gonna change after doin' this, back at the motel."

Jess shuddered to imagine what the dress looked like. "You're drunk, Edna. Did you really want to take your sorry self in that condition to the most important event of your daughter's life?"

"I'm her *mother*!"

"Then *act like it*!"

Edna snorted like a mad bull. "I thought after all the years maybe me and my own daughter could be friends. But, oh no." She jabbed a wavering finger at Jess. "Y'all hated me before you ever saw me. And you made Christina hate me, too."

"Hold on just a minute there, Kemosabe." Jess gripped the edge of the attic floor. "I don't care how drunk you are, you're not gettin' away with that. *We* didn't make Christina do anything. *You* did. *You* abused her. *You* neglected her. That girl came here starved for love. You should be glad she found it. Instead, all you're thinkin' about is yourself. If you really loved your daughter, you'd *leave her alone*! Especially on her weddin' day."

Edna pulled back her lips as if to hurl a curse—then her mouth turned to mush. She dropped her head and sobbed some more. "I just w-wanna see her get married. I just wanna know she's gonna have a happy life instead of the h-horrible one I had. That's all I've asked God for. Nothin' for me. Just for my Christina."

Oh, good grief. Jess closed her eyes. What was it about this woman? Self-centered and mean—then every

200

once in a while some hint of humanity actually popped out.

"Listen, Edna."

The woman flapped a hand at Jess and cried all the louder. The noise was worse than Penny's barking — which was still going on. Jess's headache had ratcheted up a few notches. She raised her voice. "Hey! Edna! Hear it from me —"

"I don't wanna hear *n-nothin'* from you, you hateful w-witch."

If that wasn't the pot calling the kettle black. "I'm *tryin'* to tell you somethin' nice, if you'll just shut up a minute."

Edna heaved another sob, then quieted a little, gulping breaths.

"One, Christina is very happy and will have a great life with Ben. You don't need to see the weddin' to know that. Two, after all you've done to her, I think deep down she actually *wants* to have a relationship with you. Why, I have no idea, but that's her business. Maybe if you'd quit drinkin' and flappin' your mouth all the time, that could happen. Three, I have *got* to get back to the church *right now*."

Jess turned to back down the ladder.

"Wait, wait! What about me?"

"What about you? Looks like you're stuck."

"Help me out!"

Jess chuckled. "Are you *kiddin'*? This is God's gift to my brother and his bride, far as I'm concerned. A true miracle. I'll be happy to come get you when the weddin' and reception are over."

"You can't *do* that!" Edna flapped her arms around so hard her rear end bounced against the floor. "Get me *out*!"

"Ain't happenin', Edna. And you know what? Even if you did show up at the weddin', there's a ring of cops around that church who wouldn't let you pass for all the barbecue in Texas."

Edna's eyes bugged. "They can't stop me!" She thrust a hand through her fake red hair. "I'll sue 'em! I'll sue you. I'll sue the *whole town* a Justus!"

Oh, that was a good one. "I'd like to see that, Edna, really I would. I'd just love to see you on the witness stand, trying to look all calm and nice while some lawyer"—Jess poked herself in the chest—"that would be *me*, hurls questions about your conduct that you have to answer. Do me a favor, give me that chance, I *dare* you."

Edna's cheeks flamed crimson. She sneered. "I thought your family's all about bein' *Christian*. Christians are supposed to forgive, remember?"

Ah, a new tactic—deride the opponent's faith.

"Why, Edna Day, you mean you're finally admittin' you need forgiveness? At least that's somethin'. And for your information—yes, Christians do forgive. But sometimes it doesn't come all at once. Sometimes you have to *will* it—which I'll certainly have to do in your case. And even then it doesn't mean you leave yourself open to further attack. And now"—Jess smacked the attic floor—"I am *done* talkin'."

She started backing down the ladder.

A whimper filtered through the stairwell. "But my leg hurts! What if they have to cut it off?"

"Then don't come runnin' to me."

"You can *not* leave me trapped up here!"

That did it. Jess stomped up the steps she'd just come down, sending fresh pain through her ankle. She shot Edna Day a look to kill. "Maybe I should turn out the light and close the door. That would be more like the dark closet you trapped little Christina in, wouldn't it? *Wouldn't it?*"

Edna jerked her head back. She stared at Jess, then wrenched her gaze to the floor.

Jess couldn't stand the sight of her anymore. She thudded down the ladder and hit her bedroom carpet, her ankle now a steady throb. Fast as she could she hurried to her dresser and grabbed the small velvet bag of rings. Jess whisked her high heels off the floor and opened the bedroom door. Penny rocketed in and to the bottom of the attic stairs, stiff-backed and flat-eared. Her barking rolled upward.

Not a sound from Edna.

"Penny, enough already!" Jess picked up the dog and headed again to the door. Just before closing it, she glanced back at the leg hanging from her ceiling. It was still.

Downstairs, Jess thrust Penny into the kitchen and pulled the dining room door shut. Lady Penelope howled her indignation. "Sorry, girl! Just be glad we don't have a weddin' every day."

Thank goodness. A lifetime without seeing another one would be just fine with Jess.

Outside Jess hopped into her car and raced away. Who cared if she sped? All the cops were at the church. By the time she veered into the parking lot, it was two minutes before two. She shoved into her heels, snatched the jewelry bag off the seat, and jumped out of her car.

Oww.

Teeth clenched, she hobbled for the side door of the church. She was still twenty feet away when Buddy Altweather ran around the corner. Spotting her, he pulled up short.

"Oh, hi. Wanted to make sure that was you comin' back."

"It's me." Jess didn't slow.

The Chief of Police nodded. "No sign of her. Looks like we're clear, but we'll stay at our posts."

Jess reached the door. She put a hand on the knob and turned to Buddy. "It's gonna be okay, she's not comin'."

"Oh yeah?"

"Yeah."

He eyed her. "How do you know?"

She held back a smile and shrugged. "Just a feelin' in my gut."

Jess pulled on the knob and hurried inside the church. Judy Crenshaw was pacing the hall. "Oh, finally!" She raised her arms.

"Tell Christina I'll be right there." Jess ran past her toward the men's dressing room, trying not to limp. Judy took off toward the women's area.

Jess practically flew through the open door. Ben stood before her, still drop-dead handsome in his black tux, even with his pale face. "Where have you *been*?"

"She's here, she's here!" Pogey bounced up and down. His cheeks flamed red, his freckles in dark contrast. He looked like Howdy Doody on meth.

"I got waylaid." Jess thrust the bag into Ben's hand.

"By Edna?" Ben swiveled and tossed the bag to Jake. "Tie 'em on the pillow tight, or Pogey'll send 'em flyin'."

"No I won't!" Bounce, bounce.

Jess frowned. "Pogey, you have *got* to calm down."

Ben pivoted back to her. "*Did* you see Edna?"

Oh, man, her head and her ankle hurt. Jess drew in a long breath.

"Jess!"

She clamped fingers around Ben's arm and leaned in close. "Listen to me. Edna's not comin'. So enjoy your weddin', little brother. She's not gonna spoil it."

204

He studied her. "What did you do?"

"Does it matter?"

He considered the question, drawing in the sides of his mouth. "Guess not."

Jess laid her palm against his warm cheek. "Right you are. Now this is *your* day. And Christina's. Relax and have fun."

Before he could say anything more, she turned and whisked down the hall. Judy stood at the entrance to the women's dressing room, frantically beckoning.

Throb, throb went Jess's ankle. She didn't let it slow her down.

She ran into the room to see Christina on her feet, eyes wide. "What happened?" The creases in her beautiful face told Jess she'd been imagining the worst. Jess's mom and sisters, and her two nieces all stared at her, bug-eyed.

She pulled up in front of Christina, feeling the fear rolling off the bride's shoulders. How unfair. How *wrong* an emotion—just before her wedding.

Judy closed in on Jess with a comb and large bottle of spray. "Let me fix your hair."

All the rushing-and-worry-and-anger-and-pain rose up in Jess, clotting in her throat. She gulped in air and took Christina's hands in hers. "Everything's fine. Your mama isn't comin'. I just told Ben. Now I'm tellin' you— relax. Say a prayer. Smile. This is your day, your moment. You deserve it, Christina. And nothin's gonna spoil it."

Emotions rippled Christina's expression—surprise ... relief ... back to fear. Tears formed in her eyes. "What happened to her, is she okay?"

The question startled Jess. She searched Christina's face, the words sinking through her. How amazing, the resiliency between mother and child.

Jess looked at her own wonderful mother, and gratitude swelled in her chest. Then she pictured drunken Edna Day in the attic, mad as a wet cat.

"She'll be fine. She's just … sittin' this one out."

Christina started to speak, then her face veiled, maybe against the chance of knowing too much. She gave a slight nod.

Jess squeezed her hands and stepped back. Jess's mom moved to Christina's side and slid an arm around her shoulders. "Ready, daughter?" Her voice was gentle. "How 'bout we do this thing?"

Christina mashed her lips together, then slowly raised her chin. "I'm ready. I am so *very ready*." She managed a shaky smile. "How do I look?"

"Absolutely breathtakin'," the best mother in the world replied.

Jess held back tears. "No lie, girl. Ben's just gonna choke."

CHAPTER 33

Here we go.

Just before Jamie escorted Ruth down the aisle, she peeked into the sanctuary. The place was packed with guests. Flowers decorated the front, with a small bouquet and white streamers attached to the first right pew reserved for the groom's parents. Off to the side stood Russ Barone, one of the Dearings' church friends, with a movie camera. He would film the ceremony and reception.

"Oh." Ruth smiled at Syton. "It all looks so pretty."

Taped love songs had played as the guests arrived. Ruth knew Christina and Ben had chosen each one with care. For the ceremony they'd decided on "Back at One," sung by Brian McKnight.

"Okay, Jamie and Ruth," Judy whispered. "Go."

Jamie still looked pale, but at least he was upright. Ruth took his arm and started down the aisle, Syton following. She smiled at friends and family members in the pews as she passed. They sent broad smiles back, with encouraging nods as if to say *The moment's here, and everything's going just fine.* Rita Betts, clad in glaring chartreuse and purple, bumped victorious fists together as if she alone had made the wedding possible. Syton's side of the family had arrived in town late last night. Ruth couldn't wait to hug them at the reception and introduce her new daughter-in-law.

As she and Jamie neared the pew, fragrance from the rose corsage pinned to Ruth's dress wafted to her nose—a sweet beginning to the long-awaited ceremony.

God, thank You for this.

Jamie seated her with a wan smile, then disappeared back up the aisle. Sy settled himself beside Ruth and took her hand. He squeezed it, then made a point of glancing right and left—his years-long silent message that she was the prettiest woman in the room.

Ruth squeezed back.

In her other hand she clutched a tissue. She'd told herself she wouldn't cry. But she had at both Maddy's and Sarah's weddings, so who was she fooling?

A pat on her shoulder came from behind. Ruth turned to smile at Dora and Keith. "How's Pogey?" Dora whispered. She'd been aghast to hear he'd gotten into her espresso beans.

"Energetic," Sy said.

The music faded away. For a brief moment the sanctuary was silent, save for a cough and the rustling of bodies. Anticipation trembled in the air.

The side door to the sanctuary opened. In filed Pastor Paul in his robe, followed by Ben, Jamie, Jake, Don, and Tamel. One look at Ben and Ruth's breath caught. She hadn't seen him in his tux. He'd never looked more handsome. His face radiated happiness. Ben came to a stop where Judy had instructed—was that only yesterday?—and smiled at Ruth and Syton. His thumbs rubbed across his fingers with nervous energy.

Ruth gazed down the line of men, all of them looking so dapper. Jamie seemed stable. Don and Jake were grinning. Those two. One of them had probably told a joke just before they entered. Tamel smiled at her, but Ruth sensed his underlying sadness.

Brian McKnight's song began. Ruth and Sy turned to look up the aisle. Jess was starting down, smiling and holding her white rose bouquet. Her gaze was fixed on Tamel. Ruth glanced at him. *"You're beautiful,"* he mouthed to Jess.

Ruth raised her eyebrows at Sy.

Next came Maddy, followed by Sarah. Ruth watched each of her girls, pride in her chest. Finally Tanya started down the aisle.

When she was halfway to the front, Ruth looked back toward the doorway. She could see Judy, nudging Lacey and Alex to start their procession. They looked so darling, holding their baskets. Lacey held her chin high, daintily picking up petals and dropping them on the floor one by one. Alex focused on her basket, thrusting in her little hand and drawing it out with fists of flowers. They fell in puddles at her feet.

Murmurs fluttered through the church—"Oh, look." "How *cute*."

Alex let go of another fistful, bringing a frown to Lacey's face. She elbowed her smaller cousin and whispered, "Don't throw 'em out all at once." The whisper was loud enough to carry through the church. Alex shot her a look and grabbed another fistful. She threw the petals down so hard half of them got caught on her dress. She stopped to brush them off. Lacey sent a look heavenward, then paused to help. "I *told* you."

Gentle laughter swept through the sanctuary.

209

Alex's dress finally clear of petals, the girls continued down the aisle. Lacey cast a proud smile at Sy and Ruth as she passed. Something about her granddaughter's smile in the setting of the flower-bedecked church sent a pang through Ruth's heart. What could be more important than generations of loving family—with God at the center?

Ho boy. Ruth's throat tightened.

When the girls reached the front Alex peered into Lacey's basket. "You still have some left." Another loud whisper.

"Shh." Lacey pulled it closer.

Alex reached into Lacey's basket and grabbed a handful of flowers.

"Hey, those're mine!"

Ruth could see Ben chuckling under his breath. Don and Jake shook their heads at their daughters. A frowning Maddy stepped forward and tugged on Alex's arm. She pointed past Jess to where the girls were supposed to stand. Alex and Lacey made their way to the appointed spot, Alex dropping stolen petals at the feet of each bridesmaid. When they finally reached their place and turned around, Lacey's mouth was pinched.

Fresh laughter spread from the back of the church. What now? Ruth turned to see Pogey—jitterbugging down the aisle. He gripped the pillow with white-knuckled fingers, elbows flapping and mouth in a wide grin. His feet moved in a crazed two-step completely out of sync with the love song. Flower petals kicked up in his wake.

"Oh, have mercy." Ruth let out a giggle. Syton guffawed. Ruth glanced at Sarah and Jake. They both looked fit to be tied, but the rest of the wedding party was laughing as well, including Pastor Paul.

"He should copyright that dance move," Keith said. Someone toward one of the back pews called, "Go, Pogey!"

The boy grinned all the more, the rings tied to his pillow bouncing. He jigged left and jogged right, shoulders jerking up and down. Even his head wagged side to side. The laughter swelled. Ruth thought he'd never reach his place by Tamel. When he finally did he couldn't stop moving.

"Hold still," Tamel whispered.

The dancing ring bearer managed to reduce himself to a wild sway.

The laughter took some time to die down. Ruth's sides hurt. Catching her breath, she looked up the aisle and saw the bride ready to make her entrance.

Finally, Christina's moment.

Ruth nudged Sy and stood, facing the back of the church. All the other guests rose as well.

As the love song continued, Christina started down the aisle alone, carrying her red bouquet and looking beyond gorgeous. Ruth could hear sucked-in breaths throughout the sanctuary. Even though she had just been with Christina, seeing the stunning bride now made her eyes burn. Christina's mouth curved in a little smile, face shining, with no hint of the past two days' worry. Ruth looked back at Ben. His lips were parted, his expression full of amazement. Tears glistened in his eyes.

Ruth's own tears spilled over and down her cheeks. She blotted them with the tissue.

Someone began to clap. Christina started at the sound. Another person joined in, and another, and still more until everyone was applauding. Ruth found herself clapping as well, Sy too. Cheers followed, rising to the rafters. Their joyful noise drowned out the music. Never had Ruth seen that kind of spontaneous outburst at a wedding, but it felt so right. So perfect. Christina pressed her lips together, clearly trying not to cry.

The applause continued until she joined Ben. He reached out and touched her arm. As the pair faced the preacher, the clapping died down.

With a collective sigh, the guests sat.

Ruth's mind was so full she hardly heard the ceremony. As she shot prayers of gratitude to God, Pastor Paul led Christina and Ben through their vows. Pogey danced forward to present the rings. Before Ruth knew it, the pastor was pronouncing, "May I present Mr. and Mrs. Ben Dearing!" He grinned at Ben. "I just know you're ready to kiss that beautiful bride of yours."

"Yes, sir!" Ben pulled Christina into an embrace and kissed her. As they broke apart the upbeat Queen song "You're My Best Friend" swelled through the sanctuary. New applause and cheering broke out. Ben and Christina turned toward the guests, their faces alight. Arm in arm they hurried up the aisle, their smiling wedding party in tow. The clapping fell into rhythm with the music. Ruth applauded too, until one line of the familiar song jumped out at her.

Whenever this world is cruel to me I've got you to help me forgive.

She'd never noticed that line before. Her hands slowed. She exchanged a look with Syton — *did you hear that?*

He nodded, eyes bright.

The music and final procession swept on. Pogey was the last attendant to exit. The caffeine-soaked kid danced even harder up the aisle, throwing in a few spins to the delight of the guests.

His Uncle Keith's shoulders shook. "Somebody get that boy a gig!"

CHAPTER 34

I can't believe this is happening, Christina thought as she and Ben entered the reception after the final pictures had been taken. *I can't believe I'm married.* And her mother hadn't ruined the wedding after all.

But why hadn't she come?

Christina wanted to pull Jess into a corner and ask her, but that would have to wait. First she and Ben needed to greet each person at the reception and thank them for coming. She asked Tanya to help her take off her long veil so she could move more freely. Then Christina proceeded to meet more relatives of Ben's than she could possibly remember. Aunts and uncles, and first cousins, and second cousins. Not to mention all the Dearings' friends from the church and town. Ben told Christina story after story of who this or that person was. How they'd grown up together, or he'd gone to school with their son, or mowed their lawns as a teenager, or had someone as a teacher in one grade or another. Everyone raved about Christina's dress, and how beautiful she looked, and how *happy* they were for her and Ben. The air vibrated with love and joy, Christina's own body in tune.

Pogey had not been able to keep still during wedding party pictures. And for a good half hour into the reception he kept up his dancing. All the guests' encouragement and applause certainly didn't help him calm down. Word about his chocolate espresso bean caper spread in no time. "Ah." Folks nodded their heads. "So that's it."

"Just wait till the caffeine wears off." Uncle Keith laughed. "That boy'll crash like a lazy hound on sleepin' pills."

Russ Barone said he couldn't wait to get home and copy Pogey's aisle dance into its own short video. "It's goin' up on YouTube and Facebook first thing."

Sarah and Jake made Pogey apologize for his behavior. Christina was far too happy to be mad at him. Ben chucked his nephew on the chin. "No worries, Pogey. You gave the weddin' some real personality."

When Pogey wound down he was like a puppet without strings. He found a chair, slumped over, and was soon asleep.

Forty-five minutes into the reception, Christina found herself alone with Ben for the first time. "What happened to my mother?" she whispered.

"I don't know."

"Jess didn't tell you?"

He lifted a shoulder. "No time."

Christina gazed across the room at Jess and Tamel, in deep conversation. "I'm going to go ask her —"

"What a beautiful weddin', you two!" Patricia Bigslow, one of the women at Christina's shower, swept up to them, all smiles. "I swear I've never seen a prettier bride."

After that Christina and Ben were surrounded once again by guests. Then it was time for cutting the cake, followed by tossing the bridal bouquet and garter.

"See where Jess is standin' before you turn around," Ben said to Christina, "and throw the bouquet straight at her."

Jess ended up far over to one side of the line-up. Christina arched her bouquet high to try to cover her purposeful aim. She swiveled to see the flowers headed straight for Jess, but at the last second Rita Betts, that crazy woman who ran the coffee hut, snatched them out of the air.

"Oooh!" Rita hooted. "Tamel Curd, my man, where are ya?"

Everyone clapped and hollered. Except Jess. Christina shot an apologetic glance at Ben. He held up his hands — *We tried*.

Ben had better luck with the garter. He shot it over his shoulder straight at Tamel, who caught it with ease.

"Ho boy, Jess!" Jake yelled. "Look who's next!"

Jess narrowed her eyes at her brother-in-law.

"See, Tamel, been tellin' ya for years!" Rita held up the rose bouquet. "It's destiny!"

Jess looked even more put out.

Some time later as Ben was talking to a friend, Christina caught sight of Jess and Tamel a short distance away. This was her chance. Christina headed toward them.

Jess was checking her watch. "I better get back to the house," she said to Tamel.

He cocked his head. "Why?"

Coldness ran through Christina's veins. Did this have something to do with her mother? Why else would Jess need to leave the reception early?

Christina reached Jess and looked her in the eye. "Where is my mother?"

Jess hesitated. "She … got hung up."

"What does that mean?"

Tamel spread his hands at Jess, as if to say *What secrets have you kept from me?*

"Come on, Tamel," Jess said, "you're worried enough about your dad. I didn't want to bring anything else up."

"*What* did you do?" Christina's voice edged.

"*I* didn't do anything. I just found her, that's all."

Christina's heart stalled. "Where?" She pictured her mother drunk and passed out in a ditch.

"Trapped in the attic above my bedroom."

"*What?*"

Tamel drew back his head. "In your *attic?*"

"Said she was lookin' for pictures of Ben." Jess aimed a sigh at Christina. "She was drunk. She had this frame with photos of you as a child, and she wanted to fill the rest of it with old pictures of Ben as a weddin' present. But she went too far over to the side of the attic, where there's no floorin'. One leg fell through the ceilin', and she's stuck there."

Christina stared at Jess openmouthed. "She's *still there?*"

Jess gave a slow nod.

"And you didn't help her out."

"Nope."

Christina's throat tightened. "How could you just *leave* her there?"

"Pretty easily, actually. She planned to get those pictures and hustle over to your weddin'. In her state, who knows what she would have done."

216

"But—"

"You had a beautiful ceremony, Christina. Uninterrupted. Well, except for Pogey."

"I know but—"

"I was gonna go check on her soon as the reception was windin' down. Still, I figured she shouldn't be let out of there until you and Ben drive off to the hotel, safe and sound."

"But don't you see—she's *trapped*!" The old, horrible fear rose in Christina. Her voice trembled. "She can't get *out*."

Jess's mouth opened, then closed.

Tamel touched Christina's arm. "Want me to take you over there?"

"No, I'll get Ben." Christina was already moving away. She couldn't believe this. The whole time she'd been enjoying her wedding and reception … The *whole time* …

"You don't have to go," Jess called after her. "I'll do it."

Christina swiveled back, her dress rustling. "She's been *left* there. I have to make sure she's all right."

"You still have weddin' guests."

"Jess—"

"Go, Christina." Tamel looked into her eyes as if he saw through to her soul. "You never know when you might run out of chances."

She gazed at him, shared pain flowing between them. Then she nodded. "Please tell everyone I'm so sorry I had to leave."

Christina turned and hurried toward her husband.

CHAPTER 35

The Dearings' front door was unlocked. Ben pushed it open and Christina rushed inside. On the drive from church she'd held on to the car's dashboard, conjuring images of her mother. How uncomfortable she had to be. How *scared*.

The minute Christina hit the front entry, Penny started barking. Vaguely Christina noticed the pocket door to the family room was closed. She picked up the skirt of her wedding dress and took the steps as fast as she could, Ben behind her. Upstairs she veered right. Through the doorway of Jessica's bedroom she spotted a leg hanging from the ceiling, clad in skin-tight black pants. A ladder led to the attic.

"Mom?" She ran toward the opening.

"*Christina?*" Her mother's thick voice held disbelief.

Christina reached the ladder. Ben caught her arm. "Let me go up."

"*No.*"

"You can't get through the opening, not in your dress."

"I *have* to."

She climbed as quickly as she could, feeling Ben pushing in her skirt so it wouldn't catch on the ladder's side hinges. Even so, by the time she could see into the attic, she could go no farther.

"Christina!"

She looked to her right. Her mother perched awkwardly on the floor, one leg out of sight. Thick mascara and eyeliner had dried on her cheeks, and her hair was matted down. She looked ancient and worn and pathetic.

Christina's heart curled inward. She thrust out an arm but couldn't reach far enough.

Her mother licked dry lips. "You came."

Christina nodded, throat tight.

"Why?"

"I just now heard you were here."

"But *why* did you come?"

How could she even ask that? "I couldn't leave you here."

Her mother gazed at Christina, then tore her eyes away. Slowly her head sank, and her red mouth trembled. Tears rolled down her face. "I can't feel my l-legs."

"We'll get you out. Ben can do it."

"That woman is a monster! She *left* me here."

"I'm so sorry."

Edna Day lifted her chin. She looked at Christina, her face creasing. "Would *you* have left me?"

Pictures of the beautiful wedding flashed through Christina's mind. But now to remember the music and flowers and loveliness—and all the while her mother was trapped alone in this place …

She shook her head.

Her mother looked away again and sniffed. "You should have."

Christina gripped the edge of the attic floor, feeling the wood grain beneath her fingers.

"I'd a deserved it."

Her throat burned. "*Nobody* deserves to be left like this, Mom."

"I do." Edna Day swiped at her tears. "I been sittin' here thinkin' how I did it to *you*."

She'd done far worse. The closet had been pitch black and small, the door barricaded from outside. Christina had been a *child*.

"I mean, I didn't really. Your father did. But I let him. I didn't stand up for yoooou." The last word trailed into a sob.

Christina's breath caught. Part of her wanted to scream — *It's taken you all these years to admit it?* The other part knew the pain, the helplessness of being trapped. The righteous anger, with nowhere to go but churn in the stomach. She'd lived through all that — and so much more. She'd survived it. And she wouldn't wish even a taste of it on anyone.

Her mother heaved another sob, then flexed back defiant shoulders. "I wanted to *see* your *weddin'*. I'm your *mother*, and you wouldn't *let* me."

Christina closed her eyes, the years-old weariness rising. "And what would you have done if you'd been there?"

"Just watched, that's all! How could you deny me that?"

"You're drunk."

"I am not!"

"You'd have been even worse two hours ago."

"I'd a just sat there." Edna's tone turned bitter. "In the back. Like the kitchen help sneakin' in to see the fancy party."

"No. You would have made a scene, like you always do." Christina swallowed. "You would have *shamed* me."

The word shot surprise across her mother's brow. Then her face hardened. "Sorry your own mother shames you, Christina. Get me out of here, and I'll slink on home to Austin. You'll never see me again. That's what you want, isn't it?"

Sudden cold crept over Christina's shoulders. She looked down the corridor of her life to come, imagining herself and Ben. Their home. Kids and happiness. But all the while, the hole still in her heart. Maybe with the passage of time God would heal the wound. He could heal anything. But she didn't want its edges slowly drawing inward, scabbing over until the years finally scraped it clean. She wanted the hole *filled*. With a mother she loved and who loved her back. With forgiveness. Renewal.

Would you do that for me, Jesus?

"No, Mom. That's not what I want."

Her mother grew still. She hung her head and burst into fresh tears. "I'm sorryyyy."

The word. The *word*. The one Christina thought she'd never hear. It punched her in the gut. How many years had she longed for it?

Christina couldn't speak. She could barely feel her heartbeat. She sensed Ben below her, stiff-backed, listening to everything.

"You hear me, Christina? I'm *sorry*."

Was this just the alcohol talking?

Christina pictured herself as a desperate child crying in the closet. As a teenager shoving down her wrath, planning her forever escape. As a young scarred woman incapable of trust—until Ben came along. She thought of her last few months in counseling, what she'd learned about God and how she'd grown. All that, all of the tears and betrayal and pain, had now come down to this moment. How would she respond to the apology that had come so late and in such a pitiful way?

"I hear you."

Her mother wouldn't look up.

Christina fisted her hands. Now what? Hearing her mother wasn't enough. There was so much more that needed to be said. But the words felt stuck and raw. How to even begin?

Help me, Jesus.

"And ... I forgive you, Mom."

There. She'd said it.

Christina closed her eyes, *feeling* the word inside her. It felt ...

Right.

And weary.

But there was still more to say.

Christina braced herself.

"I do that for you *and* for me, because that's what the Bible says to do. Forgiving you frees me to become ... *me.* But that doesn't mean I forget. And it doesn't mean you can keep on messing up my life." Tears filled Christina's eyes. "Thing is, I do want you in it. But you can't be if you keep drinking. If you keep being so self-centered. You abused me when I was young and helpless. You think I'd want that kind of grandmother around my children? I *can't* do that, Mom. I won't let you *near* my family if you don't change. Doesn't mean I don't love you. Doesn't mean I'd be happy about it. But I've done what I can do, and now it's up to you."

Christina took a breath. She could hardly believe what was coming out of her mouth.

223

Edna Day stayed silent.

"So ... now what?" Christina gestured toward her mother. "Is *this* the kind of life you want? Alone and trapped in your need for alcohol? Think hard about your answer, Mom, think really hard. Because if you choose that—not by what you say but by what you *do* from this moment on—then you *don't choose me.*"

Her words ran out. Tears fell on Christina's cheeks. She made no move to wipe them away.

Emotions rolled across her mother's face. She brought a fist to her mouth and rocked, back and forth, back and forth. The woman's own tears continued to flow, and her hand pressed harder against her skin until it wrinkled around her fingers. She started to moan, first low, then louder.

Faint hope trickled through Christina. In the past Edna Day would have shot back empty promises. *"Sure, sure, 'course I'll change. I already stopped drinkin', don't ya know?"*

Words of comfort rushed to Christina's lips, but she held them back. Her mother needed to face this.

Feeling the weight of her own body on one small stair, her future trembling in the attic dust, Christina watched in silence. Only then did she realize she'd begun to rock in time with the woman she'd so loved and despised.

Edna Day finally slowed. She dropped her hand. All movement stopped, but she still would not look at her daughter.

"I want *you.*"

Christina couldn't speak.

Her mother raised her head. "I mean it. I want *you.* I wanna see you be a mom. I wanna know your kids. Why do you think I drove all the way here, when you didn't invite me? I wanted to make it *right.* I wanted to start over. But everything just went so *wrong.*"

No, not again. Was she still going to blame everyone else?

"But that was my fault," her mother rushed on, as if hearing Christina's thoughts. "Mine. *I* drank. *I* acted bad to your new … family." The last word came hard. "You hear me?"

Christina managed a nod.

"You *believe* me?"

How she longed to.

"I believe you want that at this moment, Mom. I believe some things have happened inside you to bring you to say this. But right now there's no liquor around. Plus you need my help getting out of here."

"Christina." Her mother's voice was barely audible. "I'll always need your help."

A sob wrenched up Christina's throat. She leaned as far toward her mother as she could, stretching out her arm. Her mom did the same, straining, straining, until their fingers touched. They stayed in that position, both crying, as long as they could. Until Christina's arm burned and she had to lower it.

She took a deep breath. "I can't climb all the way up in my dress. Ben will have to help you out."

Her mother wiped away tears. Makeup and mascara now smeared sideways across her cheeks. "I prob'ly can't get down the steps for a while. My legs are asleep."

"I'll wait for you."

"Can he help me find pictures?" Edna Day pointed beyond her daughter. Christina turned—and for the first time noticed the half full frame lying on the floor. The photos were of her as a child. She blinked at that, trying to remember. Her parents had taken *pictures*?

"I want some of Ben as a boy. Kind of symbolic, you know? Like the two of you were always meant to be together, even when you didn't know each other yet."

Edna's mouth pulled to one side. "I brought wrappin' paper with me from home. Even remembered the scissors and tape. And a card. But I never …"

Her parents took pictures. Of her. And she was smiling. Christina couldn't quite wrap her mind around that.

"I'm sure he can help you, Mom." She looked down at her husband. He had one hand on the ladder, gazing up. His neck had to ache by now. "Is there a box up here with photos, Ben?"

"Yeah. I'll show her where they are."

Christina gave her mother an exhausted smile. "I'll see you when you get down."

"Okay."

Carefully, Christina backed down the steps to Jess's bedroom. She moved aside to let Ben go up. After some thumps against the ceiling and grunts from her mother, the hanging leg started to disappear. Christina gazed at the carpet. Plaster and debris everywhere. The detritus left behind, needing to be cleaned up, swept away.

Like her life.

Some time later her mother made it down the attic stairs, clutching photos. Ben followed, carrying the picture frame. Christina started to hug her mother, but Edna stepped back and raised both hands. "Not in your weddin' dress. You look so pretty. And I'm a mess."

Edna asked Ben to lay the frame on Jess's bed, placing the photos she'd found nearby. "See, Christina? I just need to cut these to fit. It's you and Ben. Destined to be together." She offered her daughter a tentative smile. "Bet nobody else thought of a present like that."

Christina took her mother's hand. "Only you, Mom. Only you."

CHAPTER 36

As Ben, Christina, and Edna descended the stairs to the main floor, Penny burst into a new fit of barking.

"Want to wait here a minute?" Ben leaned the picture frame against the wall. "I'll go calm her down." He headed to the family room. Behind him Edna was again exclaiming how beautiful her daughter looked.

"Hey, Penny." Ben picked the Yorkie up. She was shaking. "Shh, it's okay." He petted her soft fur. "You need to go outside? Come on." He carried her out the sliding glass door to the backyard and set her down. She trembled more in the cold as she daintily went about her business. Ben brushed the dust off his tuxedo trousers, then straightened to *breathe*.

What a day.

He didn't know how to feel about what had just happened. A small miracle? You could say that. Christina could enjoy their honeymoon better now. But Edna's promises were just words. They could be so quickly forgotten at the pull of the next drink. She'd need to conquer alcoholism—no easy task. And even if she did, mother and daughter had years of tattered history to patch. Ben could see a lot of tears and work for Christina ahead.

God, please help us all through this.

Lady Penelope trotted over and sniffed Ben's shoes. His thoughts flashed to his family, anxiously waiting at the church to hear from him. They'd promised not to come home until he gave the all-clear. By now the other guests had likely gone. Not much of a reception left once the bride and groom had disappeared.

He pulled his cell phone from a pocket and tapped his mother's number.

"Ben! What happened?"

"They talked things out, and it looks pretty good. For now. Time will tell."

"That's ... wow! I'm so *glad*! I've been prayin'."

"Thanks, we needed it. We'll still need it." Ben picked Penny up with one hand. "Edna wants to go to the motel, but she shouldn't drive right now. We're gonna drop her off and go on to Jackson. Her car's here, so somebody has to take it over to her. I don't want Christina havin' to drive it in her gown. I'll leave the keys on the mantel." He took a breath. "Edna will be goin' home tomorrow mornin'. She says just leave the car keys under the driver's seat. I don't think she's ready to see any of the family right now."

"Okay."

"Don't have Jess drive it over, just in case Edna's outside. The two of them don't need to meet up anytime soon."

A weary laugh filtered over the line. "No kiddin'. But Jess is already gone—back to the hospital with Tamel."

"Did he hear more news?"

"No, I think Henry's still stable. But that could change any time. Tamel wants to be with him."

Of course he did.

Ben stepped through the sliding glass door. He put Lady Penelope down on the family room carpet, and she trotted for her bed. The princess had dealt with enough for one day.

"Mom, thanks so much for all you've done. Dad too. I'm sorry we're leavin' this way. Not quite the send-off we expected."

"I know. But this is God at work. We'll just leave those little bags of rice at the church for someone else's weddin'."

Ben had to smile. That was his mother, positive and practical.

He ended the call and slipped the phone back into his pocket. With a final scratch behind Penny's ears, he returned to his wife and Edna.

The three of them drove to the motel in silence. Christina's gown poofed up around her, spilling over the console. When they arrived Edna got out of the car, carrying the frame and her purse with photos inside. She opened the front passenger door and leaned down "I'll leave your present at the front desk, okay? Whoever brings my car can pick it up. Hope they'll mail it to you."

"I'm sure they will."

Edna slowly straightened. "Well. Guess I better go. Hope we can talk when you get back. Have a good time."

"We will." Christina smiled. "I'll call you."

They shared a final long look before Edna closed the door. Toting her purse and picture frame, balancing on her ridiculously high heels, she held her chin up as she walked away from the car.

As Ben pulled out of the parking lot, Christina leaned back in her seat and whooshed out a sigh.

He rubbed her shoulder.

For the first twenty minutes of the drive they spoke little. Too much to say. Ben could feel Christina's churning emotions. He let her rest until they neared Jackson.

"Hey, beautiful one."

"Hmm?"

"You mad at Jess?"

Christina focused on the dashboard. "I … No. She did what I never could have done. And she saved our wedding."

Ben couldn't have left Edna Day stuck in the attic either. Much as he'd have wanted to.

"Still, just as well I don't have to see her anytime soon."

Ben had to agree with that.

Christina smoothed her dress. "Tamel's crazy about her, you know."

"I know."

"I'll bet he asks her to marry him soon. I mean, he's got to work through his own issues after his father's death and everything. But …"

Another wedding in the family? Made Ben tired just thinking about it. His parents would need a year to recover from this one. "Wonder what Jess would say."

"She's crazy if she lets him go."

"Yeah. But you know Jess."

Christina managed a laugh. "I sure do."

They reached the edge of town. Their hotel was only two miles away. Anticipation kicked up Ben's spine. He took Christina's hand.

"Know what? We got *married* today."

She shook her head. "I can't believe it."

"Me either. And now we're on our *honeymoon*."

"Yeah."

"So—no more talk about anything else, okay? Not family, not your mom. It's time to think about *us*. Right here. Right now."

Christina gave him a dazzling smile. "Just us."

He squeezed her fingers.

They reached the hotel. Ben left the car for valet parking. "Thanks." He nodded to the attendant. "We'd like help with the bags."

When Christina swept into the lobby, all eyes glued to her, murmurs of admiration flowing. Ben's heart wanted to burst. The most beautiful girl in the world was now his *wife*.

All the employees behind the check-in counter were full of congratulations. The women couldn't take their eyes off Christina's gown. As the two of them received their keys, headed for the elevator and rode to the top floor, Ben's excitement mounted. They'd done it. They'd gotten through the last two crazy days. Now they could just enjoy each other.

Outside their room, Ben used the key card to unlock the door. He propped it open with a foot. Christina moved to go inside, but he held up a hand. "Not so fast, Mrs. Dearing. We're gonna do this right." He grinned. "Ready to start the rest of our life together?"

Christina spread her arms. "So very ready."

Ben swept his bride off her feet and carried her over the threshold.

FACEBOOK.COM

Rita Betts shared a link.
December 9

Seen this video yet, y'all? It's hilarious! Already has over 3 million views. Yours Truly was there. (Even caught the bouquet at the reception!)

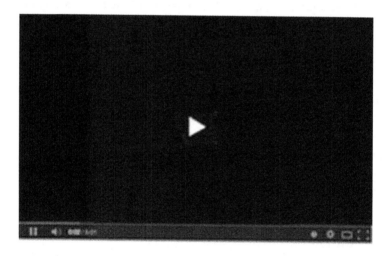

Ring Bearer Eats Chocolate Espresso Beans Before Wedding—And Can't Stop Dancing

http://m.youtube.com/3k9j3nghigK1fpLhpcM

A Note From Brandilyn

As with the first book in this series, *That Dog Won't Hunt*, readers are sure to ask me how much of this story is from my own family. You can read my answers in that book for the background on all the Dearings. As far as this particular story goes, here are three more factoids:

Remember Maddy's mixed metaphor in the first chapter—"The train has left the building"? That's a direct quote from my sister's friend Nancy Neuroth. To which my sister replied, "Is that like Elvis has left the station?"

Nobody could really fall through an attic ceiling and get stuck, you say? Uh-huh. Remember the soapy lobster scene in *That Dog Won't Hunt*? I told you that bubbly event really did happen in the home of my oldest sister. As for the fall through the attic—it also happened. Same family. No lie. Let's just say there's is a very entertaining household.

Pogey's caffeine-crazed dance down the aisle is entirely fictional. Sure would like to see that video, though. If anyone wants to create it, be my guest.

Since the release of *That Dog Won't Hunt*, my own wonderful mother, known as Mama Ruth—the inspiration for the character in this story—passed from this life into the arms of her beloved Savior. She was ninety-seven. I was not able to travel across the country in time before she died. My three sisters were with her. Mom did stop by to see me, however, on her way out of this world. Amazing, but true. You can read about it on my blog.
http://brandilyncollins.com/blog/2014/04/vision_of_my_mom_on_her_way_to_heaven/

And now, dear reader, please know I would love to hear from you. Ways to contact me:

You can email me from my website: www.brandilyncollins.com. There you can also sign up for my Sneak Pique newsletter to hear about my latest releases and book discounts. And you can read the first chapters of all my books—and check out what's coming next.
On Facebook I keep in daily contact with readers: www.facebook.com/brandilyncollinsseatbeltsuspense
On Twitter I'm @Brandilyn.

If you enjoyed this book, please consider writing an online review. I'd be very grateful.

Blessings to you all.

Turn the page to read the first chapter of *Cast A Road Before Me*, Book 1 in my Southern contemporary Bradleyville Series.

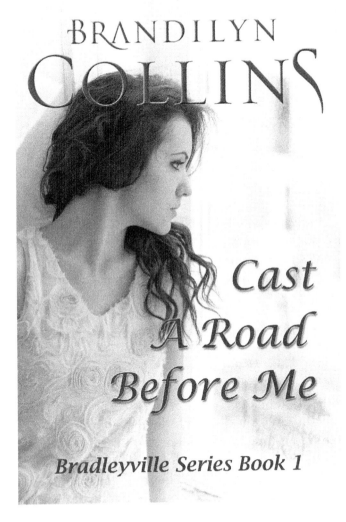

BRANDILYN
COLLINS

Cast A Road Before Me

Bradleyville Series Book 1

"4 ½ Star Gold" –RT Book Reviews

About Cast A Road Before Me

A course-changing event in one's life can happen in minutes. Or it can form slowly, a primitive webbing splaying into fingers of discontent, a minuscule trail hardening into the sinewed spine of resentment. So it was with the mill workers as the heat-soaked days of summer marched on ...

City girl Jessie Calton, orphaned at sixteen, struggles to adjust to life with her barely known aunt and uncle in the tiny town of Bradleyville, Kentucky. Eight years later (1968) she plans on leaving—following in her revered mother's footsteps of serving the homeless. But the peaceful town she's come to love is about to be tragically shattered. Threats of a labor strike rumble through the streets, and Jessie's new love and her uncle are swept into the maelstrom. Caught between the pacifist teachings of her mother and these two men, Jessie desperately tries to deny that Bradleyville is rolling toward violence and destruction.

Chapter 1

The last time I saw my mother alive, she was on her way to serve the poor.

She was wearing one of her favorite dresses, a blue cotton knit with a sash at the waist. She'd had it for years. It was her favorite not because of style, but because it was comfortable and easy to wash. "This dress will do just fine," she would say whenever I bewailed the notion that she wore it so much to Hope Center, people might think she slept in it. She was far more careful in dressing for work, starching blouses and skillfully mending old skirts so they would not betray her lack of a wardrobe. She'd add one of her three pairs of dime-store earrings, sometimes an inexpensive necklace. But any jewelry was out of the question at the Center, where it would only get in the way or, worse, remind the homeless and hungry that their needs were far beyond our own. As for the blue cotton dress, it had been spit up on by crying babies, dirtied by the spilled soup of children, even torn by the clutching hand of a frightened young mother. Mom would drag home from another long evening at Hope

v

Center, her beautiful face lined with fatigue and a thick strand of her dark auburn hair straggling out of its rubber band, and shake her head good-naturedly over the day's ruin of her dress. Then she'd wash it by hand and hang it up to dry for the next time.

I often volunteered alongside Mom at the Center. After my homework was done and her workday as a receptionist at an insurance firm was finished, we'd hurry through a simple meal, then drive to the two-story brick building in downtown Cincinnati that provided room and board to the poverty-stricken. On Saturdays I always went with her. Except that Saturday. My high school sophomore finals were the following week, and Mom insisted I stay home to study. "You stay home too," I said. "You're exhausted, and you haven't given yourself a day off in weeks. Let somebody else fill in for you just this once."

"Oh, but I can't." She smoothed my hair in her gentle way. "I promised little Jianying and a whole group of children I'd read to them today, and then I've got to teach that class on how to interview for a job. And besides, Brenda's sick, so I've got to oversee cooking dinner." Brenda Todd had founded the Center ten years previously and acted as manager. Mom had been her "right-hand woman" for eight years.

And so, on that horrific Saturday, my mother kissed me good-bye and walked out the door of our small rented house and down our porch to leave. I followed, still protesting. "Then at least let me come with you. Maybe I can help with dinner, and you can come home after the class. I'll get somebody to give me a ride home. I can study all day tomorrow."

She placed her hands on my shoulders. "No, Jessie. Stay here and study. And maybe I can find someone to work for me tomorrow. I wouldn't mind a day in bed."

She smiled, trying to hide her tiredness as she slid into our battered Chevy Impala.

I will always remember that smile. It is cut into my brain like a carved cameo. I can picture her blue dress. The paleness of her cheeks, void of makeup. The warmth of her brown eyes. She placed her worn white purse beside her on the seat, its bent handle flopping forward. Something about that old purse tugged at my heart. I thought of the long hours she was about to put in—again—for no pay. How many dresses, how many purses could she have bought had she spent as much time earning money?

Mom hadn't led an easy life herself, yet she was always thinking of others. Her husband—my father—had wandered away when I was a baby, leaving her with nothing but dark memories of his alcoholism. Years later, he was killed in a drunken fight in some bar halfway across Ohio. Her one sister lived in a tiny, remote town in Kentucky, and they rarely saw each other. And Mom had been estranged from her parents for years before their deaths. After the one and only disastrous time we'd taken a chance and visited them, I declared with all the righteous indignation a ten-year-old could muster that we'd never go back again. Within four years of that visit, my grandfather died from cirrhosis of the liver, and my grandmother from heart disease.

As Mom slipped the keys into the ignition, the smile I've held in my memory faded from her lips. Then, for the briefest of moments, her eyes slipped shut, and I watched an expression of despair spread across her features. Anxiety for her hit me in the chest. I was just about to argue with her further about staying home when her eyes reopened. She noticed me gazing at her, and the expression vanished. She smiled again, a little too brightly. The car started and she began to pull away from the curb. Her left hand came up, fingers spread. It was a small wave, intimate. "Thanks for caring," it seemed to say, "but you know I'll be fine." I lifted a hand in return and managed a wan smile back.

I sighed as I watched Mom ease down our street and turn right. Then she was out of sight. Two blocks from our house, she would turn left and begin the climb up Viewridge, which curved to become visible from where I stood.

How I wished she had stayed home to rest.

The sound of a mail slot opening clanked through my thoughts. I turned to see Jack, our mailman, pushing envelopes into the Farrells' house next door. Calling a greeting, I waited near the curb for him, shielding my eyes against the sun.

"Hi, Jessie." Jack drew near, pulling our mail from his cart. "Almost done with school for the year, aren't you?" He folded the envelopes inside a magazine and held the bundle out to me. I raised my hand to take it.

That's when the squealing began.

It was a long keening, the unmistakable sound of frantic brakes. It's not the noise alone that draws your eyes, it's the expectation of what's to follow. Jack's head jerked up. I whirled around, scanning Viewridge, and caught sight of my mother's car. Then I saw the vehicle reeling toward it, pulling a trailer. Fishtailing badly.

Dread bolted me to the sidewalk.

Time slowed, suspended in the suddenly suffocating air. In the next second it looked like Mom swerved onto the shoulder toward safety, but she had little room. Nausea seized me, even before the crash. I was watching a horror movie, thinking *"No! No!"* Then I heard the words yelled and realized they came from me.

Jack murmured a prayer. Vaguely, I registered the sound of mail hitting the sidewalk.

The crash played forever. There was the smash of impact as the truck hit the side of my mother's car, a grinding of metal and gears, the lingering screech of twisted vehicles careening to a halt. Then utter, dead silence. My feet still would not lift from the sidewalk. Screams gurgled in my throat.

My next memory puts me a block away, breath ragged with sobs, running, running ...

CPSIA information can be obtained at www.ICGtesting.com
Printed in the USA
LVOW04s2046110515

438061LV00008B/70/P